HELL HATH NO FURY

FEDERAL BUREAU OF MAGIC COZY MYSTERY, BOOK 7

ANNABEL CHASE

RE4D PALM PRESS LLC

CHAPTER ONE

"Is it really too much to ask?" Neville asked.

"Yes, as a matter of fact, it is." I dodged the flaming magical ball that my assistant tossed in my direction. The wizard and I were running through training exercises in Davenport Park. Situated near both the Susquehanna River and the Chesapeake Bay, the park is a great location for outdoor activities. It's also an ideal spot to keep an eye on 'the mound,' the nearby hillside that houses a secret portal to Otherworld, the supernatural realm. Even though the portal is dormant, it gives off mystical energy that draws supernaturals to this idyllic human town. It's the ultimate freak flag and I'm the official freak wrangler.

"You don't need to say it every day," Neville said. "It's not as though I'm suggesting we replace 'please' and 'thank you' with it. Nana Pearl always said that courtesy is the cornerstone of civilization."

I smiled wryly. "I guess that explains why my house feels more like the Wild West." I leaped to the side and rolled across the grass to avoid another ball of fire. The magical ball dissipated in the air behind me.

"You need a Nana Pearl in your family," Neville said. "She was full of lofty phrases and words of wisdom." He sighed at the memory.

I sprang back to my feet. "My grandmother is full of words of wisdom too," I said. *Move out of the way before I run you over with a lawnmower spell.* Or the more recent—*don't mix up these two potions because if you drink that blue one, you'll die an agonizing death and I'm not in the mood to clean up blood and vomit.*

"Perhaps when you're about to enter a dangerous situation," Neville pressed. "You only need to say 'it's fury time' and march in with your aggressive nature. That might even be enough to deter the demon you're facing."

"First of all, I don't have an aggressive nature. Second, if I'm about to fight a demon, a catchphrase is the last thing on my mind."

Neville rooted through his wizard bag for another spell. "If you're not keen on that one, I'm sure I can generate a few more ideas. I'm nothing if not an idea generator."

"I think we should focus more on training so you can tick the boxes in your little book."

Neville stopped rummaging to look at me. "It's not *my* little book. It belongs to the Federal Bureau of Magic. I'm merely its keeper."

"You don't have to remind me," I grumbled. "I know which master I now serve." I'd once served the FBI like the nice, ordinary human I wanted to be—until the FBI discovered that I was actually a fury with supernatural abilities. After that, they wasted no time in shipping me back home to Chipping Cheddar, Maryland in order to run the FBM outpost. The last agent in charge had been killed by a demon and they needed an immediate replacement. RIP Paul Pidcock. I never imagined I'd move back here. In fact, I'd intended to stay as far away from my family as possible for the rest of my now immortal life, but the gods had a way of making a mockery of my plans.

Neville studied the training manual. "We need to finish this section so we can move on."

"Do we have to?" I whined.

"It's like Jumanji," he said.

I didn't register the rest of his words because I was too focused on the police car in the distance. Was it Chief Fox's car or Deputy Guthrie's? I squinted, unable to tell from where I stood.

Neville cleared his throat. "I'm beginning to take your T-shirt slogan seriously," he said.

I glanced down at my light blue T-shirt that read *Easily Distracted by Dogs*. "What? I just like to state this right upfront so people aren't offended when I stop paying attention to them."

"But sometimes there's no dog," Neville countered.

I shrugged. "This is Chipping Cheddar. There's always a dog in sight." I pointed to the far side of the park. "I see a Golden Retriever right there. Very distracting. I don't think I can do any more training now that I've spotted him."

Neville eyed me with skepticism. "I don't think you were gazing dreamily at the dog, Agent Fury."

I balked. "I don't gaze dreamily."

Neville cast a glance over his shoulder. "Was that a police car that drove past a moment ago? I suppose you were hoping to touch base with Deputy Guthrie."

"Hardy har." Neville knew perfectly well that Sean Guthrie and I loathed each other. Sean and I had grown up together—he was close friends with my ex-boyfriend, Tanner Hughes. Sean had delighted in my misery after Tanner and I broke up. My thoughts trailed off as a new memory slid into place. We'd broken up because I'd caught Tanner cheating with Sassafras 'Sassy' Persimmons, head cheerleader extraordinaire. Thanks to a demon's influence over Aunt Thora, I'd recently learned that Tanner hadn't cheated of his own volition. The cruel act had been the result of a spell cast by my own family because they didn't want me in a serious relationship with a human. On the one hand, it was water under the bridge. I was no longer interested in Tanner and he and Sassy were still together. On the other hand, the violation of trust had scarred me for years and I hadn't been involved in another meaningful relationship —until now.

"Earth to Agent Fury?" Neville snapped his fingers.

"You don't have to snap," I said. "I'm listening."

"Are you?" Neville regarded me curiously. "In that case, what were my instructions?"

Okay, so my mind had wandered. That was only because training exercises were boring. If there wasn't an actual demon in front of me, I couldn't see the point of using magic or any other powers. I'd spent my life avoiding them and now I was expected to use them every day. Sometimes it was all too much.

"Your instructions were to caffeinate you," I said.

"I don't believe that's what I said."

I nodded vigorously. "You mentioned coffee. I heard you distinctly."

Neville eyed me. "Would this have anything to do with a certain chief of police holding Coffee with a Cop hours?"

"No, Chief Fox does that at Magic Beans. I was thinking we'd go to The Daily Grind." I strolled toward the wizard and gave him a firm pat on the shoulder. "Come on, Neville. You've earned a drink."

Neville still seemed distrustful. "What's wrong with

Magic Beans? I thought you'd decided to split your time between the two."

"Exactly. This is me, splitting my time." I was trying to avoid running into Chief Fox in public, especially places like Magic Beans which was owned by a perceptive witch named Corinne LeRoux. I didn't need tongues wagging if the chief accidentally brushed his hand against mine or if I laughed too loudly at his jokes. In fairness, I laughed too loudly in general.

"This is like romance roulette, Agent Fury," Neville said.

I frowned. "Romance roulette sounds like something else entirely." Neville was one of the select few that knew I was romantically involved with the chief and I hoped to keep it that way. The last thing I wanted was for my family to discover my secret and resort to magic to break us up like they did with Tanner. Although I had yet to confront my mother and Grandma about their past trickery, it was only a matter of time before I lost my temper. When things finally went cauldron-shaped, someone was going to end up dead and buried, and I didn't want that someone to be me.

The air was pleasantly warm, so Neville and I opted to walk along the promenade into town. The pathway provided a sweeping view of the bay, which sparkled in the afternoon sunlight. It was no wonder the Puritans decided to put down roots here. Who could blame them? With surnames like Burgess, Calvert, and Dorsey, the English settlers started as dairy farmers but eventually turned to cheesemaking. That decision changed the course of the town's history and was reflected in the street names and establishments to this day.

"Any plans for the rest of the weekend?" Neville asked, as we approached the entrance to The Daily Grind.

I debated whether to tell him about my date with the

chief tonight. Just because he knew about us didn't mean he had to be kept in the loop on the details though.

"The usual. Avoiding my family. Looking out the window of the attic and hoping the barn gets finished soon."

Neville chuckled and opened the door. "And here I thought I was pathetic."

The aroma of rich brewed coffee hit my nostrils and I inhaled deeply. "How about you? Have you given any thought to wading into the dating pool? There must be an app for wizards like you." I lowered my voice as we joined the line. If anyone heard me call him a wizard, they'd just think we were Potterheads.

"I don't know that I want to date a supernatural, specifically," Neville said quietly.

I leaned in closer to him. "How could you not? You'd at least have to date a human with the Sight." Neville was constantly tinkering with trinkets I might be able to use in the field. He was the magical Q to my supernatural James Bond.

We placed our order and shuffled to the side to wait for our drinks. For a Sunday, the coffee shop was hopping. Families were enjoying slices of cake with their coffee and scones with their tea. I was a bit of a coffee snob. Until the arrival of Magic Beans, The Daily Grind was the only place in town I was happy to get my caffeine fix.

"I'll secure us a table, Agent Fury," Neville said.

"Eden," I corrected him. "We're about to sit at a table together and share a cookie. I think a first name basis is acceptable."

He squinted. "We bought a cookie?"

"I may have slipped that into the order when you turned away," I said. I couldn't resist a baked good. A siren could try to lure me to a watery grave with her beautiful voice, but she'd have a much better chance of success with a plate of homemade cookies fresh from the oven.

I threaded my way through the tables, carrying a tray with our drinks and one large white chocolate chip cookie. Neville had managed to snag a small table by the window, my favorite spot.

"Your beverage, sir." I set the mug in front of him.

"This feels strange," he said. "You waiting on me for a change."

"Don't get used to it." I sank into the chair. My body didn't get tired from exertion the way a human's would, but I definitely needed to recharge after a training session.

Neville peered at me over the top of his steaming mug. "What about 'here I am to save the day?' Will that work?"

"No. Just no."

"Why not?"

"Because my name isn't Mighty Mouse," I said.

A shadow fell over the table and I glanced up to see my cousin, Meg. The pretty teenager was the daughter of Rafael, a warlock, and Julie, a werewolf. My family wasn't too excited about adding a werewolf to the family, but everyone came to love Julie, including my mother's side of the family, which was no small feat. When Meg was born and it became apparent that she'd inherited her mother's pleasant nature as well as her werewolf genes, no one uttered a single complaint, a testament to Julie's acceptance.

"Hey, Eden," Meg said. She was dressed in her usual hipster attire—a short, swinging skirt in grey and a long-sleeved black top. Her long hair was threaded into a single braid at the back.

Standing beside Meg was a girl I didn't recognize. She wasn't as effortlessly stylish as Meg. Her brown hair was pulled into a messy ponytail at the nape of her neck and she wore glasses that seemed slightly too round for her face.

"Hello there, stranger. I feel like I haven't seen you in ages," I said. "You remember Neville."

Meg smiled at the wizard. "This is my friend from school, Ava."

"Hi, Ava," I said. "Nice to meet you." I wondered whether Ava had any clue that she was hanging out with a werewolf.

"Ava moved here from Delaware," Meg said.

"My dad changed jobs," Ava added. "He's commuting to Baltimore now."

"I don't envy his commute," I said. Even though San Francisco was a busy city, I'd been able to walk or take public transportation to most places I needed to go so that I could avoid the chaos.

"Do you two have classes together?" Neville asked.

"Only one, but we met when Meg rescued me from a group of basketball players in the hallway between classes," Ava said.

"They were being jerks," Meg said, seemingly still irked by the incident. It didn't surprise me. As a werewolf, Meg was bound to have territorial and protective instincts.

"Trust me, I'm not complaining," Ava said.

"I'm sure it's not easy being the new girl in high school," I said.

"I'm used to it," Ava said with a shrug. "We've moved around a lot. Sometimes I tell people my dad is in the military, but really he changes jobs the way some people change their iPhones."

"That would be my brother," I said. Anton loved to have the latest and greatest in technology. No wonder he needed to work a side job as a vengeance demon to keep up with his love of material goods.

Meg brightened. "I babysat Olivia and Ryan last night. They're so cute."

That was surprising news. My sister-in-law, Verity, was a

druid and a doctor in town. She didn't tend to trust many people to look after her children. Then again, her main babysitters were evil witches, a vengeance demon, and a vampire, so maybe a teen wolf was a step up.

"I hope Charlemagne behaved," I said. Charlemagne is my niece's pet Burmese python that seems to think he's more puppy than snake.

"He tried to swallow my shoes whole, but I whacked him on the head with a newspaper and he slunk away," Meg said proudly.

"As long as you weren't wearing them at the time," I joked.

"We should probably get in line," Meg said. "I think three more people have come in since we got here."

"Is it always this busy?" Ava asked.

"It's Sunday," I said. "Everybody's home, plus we've got the weekend tourists taking advantage of the nice weather."

"That's how we found this place," Ava said. "We were house hunting after my dad got the job and stayed in a bunch of places. This town moved to the top of the list the weekend we visited here."

Meg threw an arm around her friend. "And I'm sure glad it did."

I couldn't help but smile as I watched them walk to the counter, arm-in-arm and giggling. They reminded me of Clara and I in high school, with our gangly arms and legs and conspiratorial style of conversation. I missed those stress-free days. Not that I missed high school though. I shuddered at the mere thought.

"Are you cold, Agent Fury?" Neville asked. "I think the sun is rather warm through the window."

"I'm fine." I gulped down the rest of my drink now that it was cool enough not to scald my tongue. "How about we call it a day? Even agents deserve free time on the weekends, right?"

We vacated the table to let a hovering couple swoop in. Tables and chairs were apparently in short supply today. As I opened the door to exit, I nearly ran smack into Chief Fox. The sexy chief of police held a chihuahua under his arm, which somehow only enhanced his sex appeal. I tried to keep my professional mask in place as I greeted him.

"Chief Fox, I thought you'd be over at Magic Beans," I said.

He grinned. "Did you now? As it happens, the line was out the door, so I decided to come here." His gaze swept the interior. "Pretty busy here too, it seems."

I patted the small dog's head. "Who's patrolling with you today?"

"This is Atticus," he said. "He's tiny but fierce."

"Hello, little fellow." Neville put his face a little too close to the dog's, prompting Atticus to bare his teeth and growl. "Oh my. Was it something I said? Should I have called him a big boy instead?"

I pressed my lips together in an effort not to laugh. "Let's not."

"Are we still on for later?" Chief Fox asked and my stomach did a deep dive.

"For our official review of cyber crime reports? Yes, absolutely." My head bobbed up and down like one of those bigheaded dolls stuck to the dashboard of Tanner's car in high school.

The chief winked at me. "Looking forward to it."

"Me too." So much.

Neville groaned as we spilled onto the sidewalk. "You two are going to have to do a better job than that if you expect to fool anyone. You might as well have sniffed each other's bums."

I frowned. "I hope you're only saying that because we just saw a dog."

Neville lowered his head. "I'm sure that likely influenced the quality of my response."

I glanced back inside the coffee shop at Chief Fox and my stomach did a happy dance. In only a couple of short hours, I had a secret date with the hottest guy in Chipping Cheddar. Life couldn't get much better.

CHAPTER TWO

Scoop de Ville was more crowded than I'd ever seen it. Even more noticeable was the fact that most of the customers appeared to be over seventy. I huddled closer to the chief. "I can see why you chose this place. No one here will remember seeing us." They'd be lucky to remember which flavor ice cream they chose by the time they returned home.

He grinned. "You're on to me. George Twisse has been hosting this senior citizens group on Sundays. There's a bus that transports them over and picks them up after two hours. It's called the Sundaes on Sunday program."

"Where's Atticus?" I asked, as we joined the line of walkers and wheelchairs.

"Back at the rescue center," he said. "I only had him when I was on-duty."

"Any takers?"

"Not yet, but I feel confident," the chief said. "He put on a good show today."

"How does Achilles feel about your involvement with other dogs?" I teased. The chief had adopted the pug after taking him out on patrol as part of his animal adoption efforts.

"He's cool with it," Chief Fox said. "He wants other dogs to find their forever homes too."

I inched closer to him as the line progressed. "I appreciate that you're not trying to push us out into the open."

He studied me. "I have no interest in you leaving your job, Eden, especially now that I know what you really do. I'd be useless in your line of work."

"That's not strictly true," I said. "Your skills are transferable."

"I'll be sure to put that on my resume." He turned his attention to the large menu on the wall behind the counter. "What are you thinking?"

"What thought is required? If there's chocolate, nothing else exists."

"I'm a fan of pistachio myself," he said.

I wrinkled my nose. "Is that an Iowa thing?"

He laughed. "Why do you assume everything you dislike is an Iowa thing?"

"I don't," I objected. "I've just never met anyone with a penchant for pistachio."

"I guess in San Francisco they liked more decadent flavors like creme brûlée."

I gave it some thought. "My partner Fergus preferred vanilla bean. He wasn't the most adventurous guy, despite his job."

"Not even hot fudge on it?"

I shook my head. "Nope."

The elderly man in front of us turned slowly to look at us. "Plain vanilla? Good grief. I bet he only did it missionary style too." He smiled. "I thought I heard your voice, Chief."

Chief Fox shook the old man's hand. "How's it going, Caleb? I didn't realize that was you ahead of us."

"I wouldn't notice me either with a pretty lady like that beside me." Caleb offered his hand to me. "Glad to see the chief is settling in nicely."

"I'm a federal agent," I said quickly. "We're work colleagues."

Caleb winked. "If I had a work colleague that looked like you, I wouldn't be getting much work done."

"Mr. Felton, it's your turn," a middle-aged woman called from further up the line. She seemed to be in charge of wrangling the seniors.

Caleb cupped his hands around his mouth. "The works. If I die tonight, I want to know I lived life to the fullest."

The woman heaved a sigh. "Mr. Felton, no one is dying tonight."

"I might," he said. "You never know when your time is going to be up. All part of the fun."

The woman gave him a patient smile. "You're perfectly healthy."

"I won't be after I inhale a sundae. My arteries are starting to clog in anticipation."

Chief Fox clapped the old man on the shoulder. "I'm right here if you find yourself in need of emergency services."

We finally placed our order and snagged a small table in the corner, away from the window.

"Why no cone?" he asked. "I pegged you for a waffle cone kind of girl."

"I don't like when it drips on my hands." I spooned the smooth chocolate ice into my mouth and savored the rich flavor.

He chuckled and held up his hand that clutched the cone. "You mean like this?" Green flecks of ice cream dotted his hand. "I don't mind licking it off." He held his hand closer to my mouth. "Unless you'd like to do the honors."

I recoiled. "That would involve tasting pistachio. No thanks."

"I'll be sure to refrain from using my pistachio body spray now that I know." The chief reached into his pocket. "Okay, now I need a napkin." He frowned as he leaned to the side and pulled a white square from his pocket.

"What's the matter?" I asked.

"I could've sworn I had my pocket watch in there earlier."

I stifled a laugh. "Pocket watch? Boy, you really did choose the right crowd to mix with."

"It belonged to my grandfather years ago," the chief said. "I used to play with it as a kid, so he left it to me in his will."

I felt guilty for laughing at him when the watch had sentimental value. Some secret girlfriend I was. "When's the last time you remember seeing it?"

"Earlier today," he said. "In the coffee shop when I took coins out of my pocket for the tip jar."

"If you want, we can retrace your steps when we're finished. I'll help you look for it."

His tongue darted out and swiped the mound of ice cream. "It's fine. I bet I left it on my desk at work and forgot."

I devoured the last of my ice cream. "I'm happy to look there too."

His lips curved into a sensual smile. "Now that I think about it, I might have left it in my bedroom. Under the covers."

I licked the remnants of chocolate from my spoon. "Nice try."

He dabbed the tip of his ice cream cone on my nose. "Let's see how long your tongue can stretch."

I snatched the napkin from the table and wiped it off.

"Spoilsport," he said.

"I don't want to strain it too early in our date," I said. "It would be a shame for you to miss out."

Desire rippled across his handsome features. "You know, we can walk to my place from here. All side streets too. It's dark. No one will see us."

The prospect of being alone with Sawyer Fox in his house held massive appeal right now. Still, I hesitated. "It might be a bad idea."

He grinned. "I didn't say it was a good idea."

We ditched the remains of our ice cream and headed to the door. Caleb gave us an enthusiastic thumbs up as we passed by.

"Maybe we should think about buying a carton of Ben & Jerry's next time and eating it at your house," I said.

We rounded the corner and ambled down the quiet side street. There were no streetlights and the only sound was a television from the house across the street with the window open.

"We'll be dating ninjas," he said. He cut me a glance. "Still, I'd prefer to be able to take you out. It won't feel much like a real relationship if we're constantly stuck in my house."

"Then it'll just feel like we're already married." I clapped a hand over my mouth. It was meant to be a joke, but now I worried it sounded like I was getting way ahead of myself.

To my relief, he chuckled. "That's what I like about you, Fury. Always thinking ahead." When he reached for my hand, I didn't shrink away. It felt nice. Natural. Like our hands were always meant to be joined.

"What if someone sees us?" I whispered. We turned down the next street and I surveyed the area for potential witnesses.

"No one's going to see us," the chief said. "I jog along these streets all the time and it's a snoozefest. No one's ever around." He tugged me closer. "We can even do this." He kissed me softly on the lips and I practically melted.

I placed a hand on his chest. "Let's not tempt fate."

"Why not? Fate sure is tempting me." He sauntered up the walkway to his house, a modest white bungalow with a wide front porch, black shutters, and a cheerful red door.

Achilles greeted us when he opened the front door. The chief immediately bent down to rub the dog's back. "Hey there, buddy. Did you miss me?"

The pug panted as though he'd just finished a marathon. I crouched down to scratch the dog behind the ear. He was adorable and I liked that he and Princess Buttercup played nicely together. If you're going to date someone, you prefer that your kids get along.

"I straightened up," he said. "Just in case."

"I'm glad I said yes," I told him. "I'd hate for you to have gone to any trouble."

He shrugged. "I figured I'd go out and find another lucky lady to bring home."

I shoved him. "Bite your tongue, Sawyer Fox."

He laughed. "You know I only have eyes for you, Eden."

I stared at him for a long beat before I forced my gaze away. We'd only walked in the door. It was too soon to start ripping off clothes—not that I planned to be naked with him tonight. At some point tonight I'd be naked, but at home in my bathroom. Alone.

I took a moment to digest the interior and get my mind out of the gutter. Brown leather sofa. Recliner where Achilles had chosen to settle. Reasonably sized television that suggested he watched occasionally but not obsessively. His house was an accurate reflection of him—tidy without feeling rigid. I knew if I spilled something on the rug, he wouldn't have a heart attack.

"Care for a drink?" he asked.

I clutched my stomach. "Too full to fit anything else."

His eyes creased at the corners. "Same." The chief

17

extended a hand. "How about we search for my pocket watch?"

I entwined my fingers with his. "How many years have you been using that line?"

"First time. I like to keep things fresh."

"Do you want to run over to your office now and look for it?" I asked. "I don't mind."

He squeezed my hand. "Are you nuts? I finally have you in my house. Do you think I'd be foolish enough to leave? No pocket watch is worth that sacrifice."

I didn't object as we drifted toward the sofa. He tugged me closer to him and I inhaled the scent of fresh pine and sea salt. His lips found mine and I sank against his firm chest, wrapping my arms around him.

"This is nice," he murmured.

"As long as no one spotted us coming in here," I said. "How nosy are your neighbors?"

"Relax, Eden. I triple-checked that the coast was clear." He rested his forehead against mine. "It's bad enough we have to sneak around. Let's not make a mountain out of a molehill."

I bit my lip. I couldn't tell him that it *was* a mountain when it came to my family. He thought the only reason I cared was the strict FBM regulations.

"I'm sorry," I said. "It stresses me out, that's all."

He grinned. "You know what's good for unwinding?"

I played with the button on his shirt. "Gin?"

He cupped the back of my head and kissed me, firmly and deeply. I closed my eyes and enjoyed the sensation. I was glad I hadn't strained my tongue on ice cream. This was much better.

We moved our tongue tango to the sofa and I collapsed against a pillow. Kissing him was like being snuggled under a cozy blanket that heated my entire body. Suddenly I heard a snapping sound and the air in front of me changed. My face rubbed against a more abrasive surface.

"You really need to shave," I said. I opened my eyes to smile at him—and screamed.

Chief Fox was gone. In his place was a small reddish-brown fox.

Achilles began to bark wildly. I scampered away from the fox and fell off the sofa.

"What's going on?" I shrieked and leaped to my feet. The fox stared at me and I could see the confusion in his dark eyes.

Achilles jumped from the recliner and came over to investigate, growling as he moved.

"Sawyer, is it you?" I crept back to the sofa and kneeled beside him. The fox said nothing. He turned and hid under a pillow, his tail billowing behind him.

Achilles seemed confused, barking and then stopping. I lifted the dog and carried him to the laundry room, shutting the door between us. Whatever was happening, it was best to keep the two animals apart.

I returned to the sofa, my heart thundering in my chest. Anger simmered beneath the surface as I realized what likely happened. My family must've discovered our secret and acted accordingly. I knew we shouldn't have gone anywhere in public. It had been foolish on my part.

"They won't get away with this," I said. I clenched my hands, ready to spit fire. I lifted the pillow to address the fox. "Listen, Sawyer. I need you to stay here. Do not leave the house for any reason. I'm going to take Achilles somewhere safe and get you turned back as soon as I can."

I kissed the top of his furry head and hurried into the kitchen. I filled a bowl with water and set it on the floor. Then I rummaged around for appropriate food. He had a full belly right now, but he'd be hungry come morning. I located blueberries and carrots and dumped them into another bowl, setting it beside the water.

"I promise I'll be back," I called. "Please stay put for your own safety." I retrieved Achilles from the laundry room and held the pug against my chest, speaking to him in soothing tones. "We're going for a ride, buddy. Try to stay calm."

Under the cover of darkness, I spread my black wings—one of my nonrefundable gifts from the gods—and flew to Neville's place to deliver the dog. Desperate times called for desperate measures. The wizard was understandably shocked by the arrival of the pug, but he took it in stride. I flew back to my car in town and drove home to Munster Close, my hands shaking on the wheel. I had to take care with how I approached this with my family in the off chance they weren't responsible. I could picture my mother now, snickering behind her white wine spritzer over the clever choice of a fox.

I parked in front of the house and hurried up the steps to the porch. Princess Buttercup was waiting for me when I opened the door. Although she looked like a well-fed Great Dane to humans, she was actually a hellhound I rescued from an unhappy fate outside the entrance to the underworld.

I stroked her head. "Can you tell I'm seething? Yes, I am." I spoke in a singsong voice so as not to upset her. The last thing I needed was a hellhound spewing fire and brimstone in the farmhouse on my behalf.

I marched into the kitchen and found my great-aunt alone at the table sipping a cup of hot water with lemon and honey. She leafed through a magazine with mild interest.

"Where is everyone?" I asked, trying to maintain a casual air.

She glanced up. "Good evening, Eden. Your mother's on a date and your grandmother went to bed early. She was tired from all that screen time earlier."

"More Little Critters?" Grandma was obsessed with a game app on her phone that involved walking around town and collecting creatures.

"There was an event downtown today," Aunt Thora said. "I think she was on her feet too long."

Hmm. If they weren't even together, it seemed unlikely that they were responsible for the chief's transformation. I needed more information, so I slid into the chair across from Aunt Thora.

"Were they together earlier today?" I asked.

Aunt Thora absently brought her cup of tea to her lips. "They live here. Of course they were." She turned back to her magazine. "They were both here for breakfast, but your grandmother was gone most of the day."

Although it could have been an attempt to create an alibi, I didn't think the witches in my house were responsible. Aunt Thora wasn't a great liar and she'd know if they'd been up to something. She'd also be aware if they knew about the chief and me. The fear would be written all over her face.

"Who's Mom out with tonight?" I asked. I had to feign interest or I'd burst with anxiety over the chief's trans-formation.

"Some banker named Rudy." She placed a lemon wedge into her mouth and sucked out the remainder of the juice.

"Did you know that lemons are actually a cross between bitter oranges and citrons?" I asked. "They're a freak of nature."

Aunt Thora looked at me askance. "I beg your pardon?"

"It's true," I said. "And I'm sure you'll say that the simple fact doesn't stop them from being the most glorious of all the fruits."

The older witch stared at me. "Do you get all your infor-mation from the internet?"

"What makes you ask that?"

"I'm fairly certain that lemons are native to India," she said. "While the Meyer lemon is a hybrid from the United States, lemons in general are not what I would consider freaks of nature."

Huh. Consider me schooled.

"Do you know where my mom went on her date?" I asked. I tried to calculate whether I had enough time to do a quick sweep of her room, just to be thorough. With Grandma asleep in her room, I couldn't check there.

"Baltimore by the sound of it. She said not to be alarmed if she didn't come home tonight, as though we'd ever worry about her safety." She snorted.

"No, definitely not." I pretended to yawn. "It's been a long day. I think I'll turn in too." I started toward my mother's room.

"Eden, how tired are you?" Aunt Thora called. "The attic is that way." She jabbed a thumb over her shoulder.

I gave an awkward laugh. "I'm clearly exhausted." I climbed the attic steps to my makeshift bedroom. "Alice," I hissed, but there was no response. "Alice!"

"You rang?" Alice Wentworth drifted into view. The ghost had inhabited what had once been her family's farmhouse since her death over two hundred years ago.

"Can you do me a favor? I need you to scope out my mother's room and Grandma's room and see whether there's any evidence of a spell."

Alice reeled back. "You want me to voluntarily sneak around their bedrooms? Do you think I have a death wish?"

"You're already dead."

Alice seemed unpersuaded. "Even so."

"My mother's out and Grandma's asleep. Besides, it's not like she can see you if she wakes up." The ability to see and speak to Alice was one of my fury powers, not a witchy one.

"Maybe not, but sometimes I get the sense that she can feel me." Alice shuddered. "It's creepy."

Leave it to my grandmother to creep out a ghost.

"Alice, please. Chief Fox has been turned into an actual fox and I need to know if my family is responsible and how to reverse the spell."

Alice gasped. "A fox? You don't say. Why would they do that?"

"Revenge for dating a human behind their backs."

"I haven't heard them talk about magic in the past few days," Alice said. "It's been mostly Little Critters this and Little Critters that. And your mother was obsessing about which lingerie to wear on her date with Rudy."

I pressed my hands against my ears. "That's enough of that."

Alice hovered by the wall. "I'll take a quick look and see if there are any remnants of a spell lying around. Will that suffice?"

"Yes, thanks." While I waited, I stripped out of my clothes and into shorts and a T-shirt for bed.

Alice returned a few minutes later, her head poking up from the floorboards and startling me. "Nothing."

"Nothing at all? No spell book? No herbs?"

The ghost shook her head. "The only evidence of magic was your mother's cosmetic collection on her vanity."

"That's not magic, that's a miracle," I said.

Alice smiled. "What will you do about the chief?"

"Nothing tonight. He's safe at home for now. I just need to think." I sat on my mattress and rested my elbows on my thighs, trying to drum up theories. "He's too new to have enemies in town, don't you think?"

"From the sound of it, everyone adores him."

"What's not to adore?" He was charming, funny, hot as

hell. My cheeks warmed as I remembered our date—the part before he turned into a woodland creature.

"Careful, Eden," Alice said. "You walk around with a dreamy expression like that and your family will definitely suspect something."

I rubbed my cheeks. "I'll go brush my teeth. I want to be up bright and early to figure this out."

By the time I returned to the attic, my yawns were genuine. I climbed under the sheet and hoped that the chief wasn't too frightened. I'd left him food and water and would go back to check on him in the morning. Beyond that, there was nothing else I could do.

"Good night, Sawyer," I whispered into the darkness. "Sleep well." I licked my lips and was pleased to discover that I could still taste him. I found this fact oddly reassuring as I drifted off to sleep.

CHAPTER THREE

"SORRY I'M LATE." I hurried toward our usual booth in Gouda Nuff, the diner where I regularly congregated with my best friend Clara Riley and my frenemy, Sassy. To be fair, Sassy had grown on me since my return to Chipping Cheddar. Her friendship with Clara had opened my eyes to another side of the superficial beauty and, now that I knew the truth about Tanner, it made me feel more disposed to like her. I shouldn't, given that the spell was done to Tanner and not Sassy. She exercised free will when she got down and dirty with my boyfriend. Still, she'd changed in the years since high school and so had I.

"Your omelette should still be hot," Sassy said.

I slid into the booth beside Clara and set my napkin on my lap. "Ooh, you got me spinach and feta. Thanks."

Clara winked at me. "I think I know you well enough to order for you."

"I have complete faith in you." I sucked down iced tea through a metal straw, just one of the diner's efforts to become more environmentally friendly.

"I'm going out on a limb and blaming your family for

your tardiness," Clara said. Not only was she a human gifted with the Sight, she was also an empath with the ability to feel others' emotions. As much as I disliked my fury powers, I thought Clara's ability was worse in many ways. She found it difficult to get too close to people. The resulting emotions were sometimes too overwhelming, so the best method of protection was limited involvement.

"You wouldn't be wrong. Anton dropped off Ryan on his way to an appointment, and then decided to linger. He wasn't in much of a hurry." I'd debated telling my brother about Chief Fox's transformation to get his insight. Ultimately, I decided against it. If my family wasn't behind the change, I needed to keep it quiet. I couldn't risk the entire town discovering that their head of law enforcement was now a furry creature.

"I saw you and Chief Fox last night," Sassy said with a sly smile. "Working late on a Sunday, were you?"

"Did you know that Scoop de Ville hosts senior citizens on Sundays?" I asked. I snatched a fry off the plate in the middle of the table and swiped it with ketchup before popping it into my mouth.

Sassy wagged a finger. "Don't try to change the subject."

"Is Tanner traveling this week?" I asked, ignoring her directive. I desperately wanted to confide in Clara about what happened to the chief, but there was no way I could manage it while Sassy was with us. The realization that I was keeping another secret from Sassy triggered my guilt complex. It was bad enough that the secret involving Tanner was such a doozy. Unfortunately, I couldn't spill those magic beans without telling Sassy more than she was equipped to handle. It was best to keep her ignorance of the supernatural world firmly in place.

"He's back on Wednesday evening," Sassy said. "I scheduled most of my appointments for the next three days, so that I can be around on Thursday and Friday when he's home." As an advertising salesperson for *The Buttermilk Bugle*, the local newspaper, Sassy used her considerable charm to land advertising contracts for an otherwise dying institution.

"You're more accommodating than I'd be," Clara said. "That schedule interferes with binge-watching my favorite shows."

Sassy nibbled on the end of a fry. "Gee, I can't imagine why you're still single." She swiveled her head in my direction. "The question is—are you?"

"Nice try," I said.

"Where'd you sleep last night?" Sassy eyed my purple top. "You weren't wearing that when I saw you yesterday, so you must've changed." She gripped my arm. "Unless you're already keeping clothes at his place. Are you?"

"That's a no." The only thing I was keeping at his place was a bowl of food and water. I'd gone by earlier to check on him. He'd looked so mournful that I couldn't bear to stay very long. I promised him that I was doing everything in my power to turn him back. He'd curled up in a ball and tucked his head underneath the fluff of his tail.

"Well, if you're not getting it on by now, you should be," Sassy said. "As much as it pains me to admit it, you two have incredible chemistry."

"Thank you for your support," I said.

"Seriously," Sassy persisted. "You're both single. He's hot and you're vaguely attractive. What's the problem?"

"You know what the problem is," I said. "FBI regulations. I can't date the chief of police. It's a conflict of interest."

"Like they'll come and check on your love life," Sassy said with a halfhearted roll of her eyes. "They have more important things to do like..." She trailed off. "What does the FBI do again?"

"Arrest people that annoy us," I said, flashing a bright smile.

"I've got a meeting with the mayor in half an hour to ask for access to the town archives," Clara said, in an effort to change the subject.

"Big story?" I asked. Clara was a reporter for the paper, which is how she and Sassy became friends during my absence. Although I'd reacted poorly to the change at first, we were all in a much better place now.

"I convinced Cal to let me write a story about the secret club for Puritan families," Clara said. "Ever since you mentioned it, I haven't been able to stop thinking about it."

"I can ask…" I nearly said 'Alice,' but quickly stopped myself. Sassy had no idea that I could communicate with our resident ghost. "Grandma. She's as old as the hills. She might know something."

Clara suppressed a smile. She knew perfectly well that I meant Alice. "Any help you can offer would be great. I figure town records are a good starting point."

"It helps that Mayor Whitehead isn't from here original-ly," I said. "She won't have the same desire to keep the club secret." Wilhelmina Whitehead moved from Sarasota for her husband's job and fell in love with our idyllic town, so much so that she decided to run for mayor.

"Who would want to belong to a stuffy old club for Puritans anyway?" Sassy asked. "What do they do—sit around judging people for their loose morals?"

"That's pretty much half my neighborhood," Clara said. "No club required."

"It's probably a status symbol," I said. "A way of feeling superior to others." I'd learned about the club from Farley Twisse, a descendant of one of the original Puritan settlers of Chipping Cheddar. His family had once owned acres of waterfront land and Farley now owned the miniature golf course with a view of the bay. He'd told me that other descendants of the Puritan families were in a secret club. Farley wasn't a member because, like his father, he was more interested in being a good businessman, which meant inclusivity over exclusivity.

"I want to know why it's a secret," Clara said. "What do they do in their meetings that it has to stay private? Is there a secret handshake?"

"I'm surprised Cal didn't know more about it," I said. The owner of *The Buttermilk Bugle*, Calybute Danforth, also hailed from a founding family and he and Gilbert Twisse had been friends.

"You know Cal," Clara said. "He did that thing with his eyebrows, but otherwise seemed disinterested."

"At least he doesn't have you covering the middle school soccer game," I said.

Clara gnawed on a fry. "That's why I suggested the story. If he's not going to assign me interesting ones, then I figure I'd better start rooting them out for myself."

"Good for you," Sassy said. "Spoken like a true witch."

Clara and I exchanged panicked looks. "Excuse me?" I said. "What's that supposed to mean?"

Sassy flicked a dismissive finger. "It's not an insult. It's a feminist thing. Being a witch means hexing the patriarchy and refusing to be marginalized. It's totally a compliment."

The relief in Clara's eyes reflected my own. "Cheers to that," Clara said, and raised her glass of iced tea. Sassy and I tapped our glasses to hers.

"We're all witches," Sassy said. Her smile quickly turned into a frown. "I can't say it in front of Gale though. She got an attitude when I mentioned it to her."

I laughed. "Tanner's mom is definitely not someone willing to embrace her witchy side. She worships Tanner too much to want to overthrow the patriarchy." According to

Gale Hughes, Tanner could walk on water, turn water into wine, *and* bring home the bacon.

Sassy played with the coleslaw on her plate. "I worry that I've fallen into the same trap. I need to be more of a witch."

"You don't worship Tanner," Clara said.

"No, but I do have a tendency to let him have his way all the time," she said. "I'm much tougher when it comes to other people. When it's Tanner, I sort of cave."

"It's different when you love someone," Clara said.

"Maybe, but should it be?" Sassy gulped down the rest of her water. "I mean, everything's fine. I'm not trying to act like it isn't." She wiped her hands on her napkin. "Forget I said anything."

"I like the witch idea," I said. As long as there was no black magic involved, I was fully on board with witches of any and all varieties.

"We could start our own secret coven," Sassy said. I could tell by her tone that she meant it as a joke. If only she knew.

The door opened and a familiar sight entered the diner. "And now I wish I hadn't eaten so much because I want to hurl," I said.

Deputy Sean Guthrie immediately zeroed in on our booth and he sauntered over. "How's it going, ladies?"

"How's it going with you, Sean?" Sassy greeted him. She and Sean had remained friendly since high school, whereas the red-headed deputy and I were barely tolerant of each other.

"Had to order my lunch to go," he said. "Calls are keeping me busy and the chief is MIA."

Clara shot me a quizzical look. "MIA?"

I snapped my fingers. "Oh, right. I should've told you."

Sean narrowed his eyes. "Told me what?"

"Chief Fox was in to see my sister-in-law," I said. "He's

pretty sick and Verity said it's highly contagious so he needs to be left alone until he recovers."

Sean scratched the back of his head. "What does he have?"

"That's confidential," I said. "Can't breach privacy laws, Deputy Guthrie. You should know better than that."

"You just told me he was sick and it's contagious," he shot back.

"There are exceptions for emergencies and this qualifies," I said. When it came to Sean, the more authoritative you sounded, the more likely he was to back down. One of several reasons he'd never become chief.

He grimaced. "Well, I hope he gets better fast because this job definitely requires more than one person." His phone buzzed and he groaned. "It's been nonstop." He clicked the screen and held the phone to his ear. "Deputy Guthrie."

Clara pressed on my foot under the table and I knew she was dying to know what was going on.

"Later," I mouthed.

Sean tucked away the phone. "Looks like I'll be eating in the car. Some woman's hysterical about an enormous snake on the loose in her yard."

I froze. "How enormous?"

"She said she, her cat, and her refrigerator were likely in danger."

I wiped my mouth with a napkin. "I'm coming with you," I said. Charlemagne was big enough to strike the fear of the gods into anyone. Given that they'd recently moved in to their renovated home, it was possible that the snake had escaped and was trying to find his way back to my mother's house.

"I don't need a federal agent to accompany me on official calls," he said. "I'm not the chief."

"No, you're definitely not," I said, "but if this snake is

Charlemagne, you're going to want me there. He won't answer to you."

"I don't need him to answer to me. I'll call Animal Control and let them kill it."

"On second thought, he likes the taste of gingers," I said. "Maybe I'll leave you to hunt him down on your own."

Sean didn't seem to know whether I was joking. I decided to put him out of his misery. No matter how much I wanted to torture him, I needed the deputy in good condition while the chief was indisposed.

I tossed cash on the table. "Sorry to eat and run, girls, but I'm clearly needed. We'll catch up later."

Clara gave me a pointed look. "We'd better."

I stood and faced the deputy. "Do you have any Cheez-Its?"

Sean scrunched his face. "Do I look like I'm twelve?"

"More like fourteen because of the acne." I paused. "I didn't realize snack foods had an age limit."

"Why do you care?"

"Charlemagne loves Cheez-Its. I thought we could leave a trail like breadcrumbs and see if it's him."

"We can stop at the store on the way," Sean said. He aimed a finger at me. "But you're paying."

I held up my hands. "Relax, Deputy Huckleberry. I'll fork over the big bucks for the bait."

Clara leaned on her elbows and regarded us. "You know, there are a lot of odd couple, buddy cop movies I'd pay good money to watch, but this pairing isn't one of them."

Sean took a step away from me. "No need to worry about that. This is official business only. If it goes smoothly, I won't issue a citation for the rampaging snake."

"Charlemagne doesn't rampage," I said indignantly. "He's more of a smooth operator. He can sneak up on you better than a ninja. He likes to steal my niece's butterscotch candies."

Sean stared at me. "The snake likes candy?"

"He's also partial to the strawberry ones with the jelly center," I continued. The more horrified he looked, the more I wanted to keep talking. "They crunch just like a cockroach but with a strawberry flavor. What's not to love?"

"Remember that time he got into your grandmother's laxatives?" Clara threw her head back and laughed. "What a disaster!"

My stomach turned at the memory. "I hadn't seen my mother that angry since she and my father's fight over their divorce settlement."

"Your grandmother wasn't happy either," Clara said gleefully. "She was still constipated."

The seat vibrated and I realized that Sassy was shaking with laughter. "Now I want a pet snake," she said.

Sean cringed. "None of that is encouraging. We should probably hurry."

CHAPTER FOUR

SEAN TOOK the lead and knocked on the door of the hysterical middle-aged woman. Half a face appeared in the opening crack. "Ms. Worthington, I'm Deputy Sean Guthrie. You called about a snake."

"It's Eloise. Calling me Ms. Worthington makes me sound old, which I'm not. A few extra pounds and mood swings are totally normal for a woman of any age." The gap widened as she yanked the door open the rest of the way. "Come in. Hurry." She peered around us. "I think it's lurking." She ushered us inside and slammed the door in a hurry.

"Can you describe the snake?" I asked.

She looked me up and down. Her blond, chin-length hair had a slight wave to it and her green eyes were so pale they reminded me of a stained-glass window.

"Who are you? Animal control?"

"Eden might be the owner of the snake," Sean said. "I thought it best to have her with me."

"Technically, my niece is the owner."

"How old is your niece?" Eloise asked.

"Olivia is five going on fifty-five," I said.

Eloise's jaw disconnected. "You let a child keep that thing as a pet? Are you trying to become a YouTube sensation the hard way?"

"Charlemagne is harmless," I said. Unless you tried to take away his toy. Then you needed to watch for fangs.

"What if it isn't your snake?" Eloise asked. "Did you call your niece and see if he's missing?"

"She's at school," I said. No one was home to check on Charlemagne right now. "Now, where did you last see this snake?"

Eloise pointed behind us. "On the front lawn by the step. It was watching me, waiting for its moment to strike."

Okay, Eloise seemed to have indulged in a bit of day drinking. Understandable for a weekend or if you lived with evil witches, but today was Monday and Eloise appeared to live alone.

I turned to Sean. "How about you stay here with Eloise and I'll take a look around the yard?"

"Sounds good to me," Sean said. No surprise there. Any guy afraid of his own shadow was probably afraid of snakes too. How he'd managed to become a deputy, I'd never know. Chief O'Neill must've seen something in the soulless ginger that escaped me.

I slipped outside and surveyed the front lawn. There was no sign of movement. I walked the perimeter of the yard, occasionally calling Charlemagne's name. I even shook the bag of Cheez-Its for good measure. I rounded the corner of the house and inspected the backyard. It was compact and tidy, with a bistro table and two chairs on the patio. Cheerful potted plants lined the perimeter of the pavers. It was then I noticed that a pot on the end had been knocked over. Although it could've easily been due to a gust of wind, it was worth checking. I peered at the fallen pot and saw where the soil had spilled into the grass—along with something else.

"What's that?" I crouched down to examine the discovery. Snakeskin. Unfortunately, it didn't match Charlemagne's.

I picked up the snakeskin and returned to a standing position. Somehow, I had a feeling that Sean wouldn't be excited about taking snakeskin back to the office as evidence.

I walked the length of the backyard before returning to the front of the house where Sean and Eloise were talking. A Siamese cat threaded her way through Eloise's legs as she spoke.

"I found this," I said, holding up the snakeskin. "Otherwise, there was no sign of the snake."

Sean squinted at the evidence. "Doesn't look like anything special. It's probably just a garden snake."

"Technically, they're garter snakes," I said.

Eloise balked. "It can't have been a garter snake. That thing was huge."

"Look, Ms....Eloise. The chief is sick and I've got more important things to do than show up because a lady is scared of a snake."

Eloise fixed him with a hard stare. "Pretty sure all your socks are in the laundry, lover boy. You might as well make yourself useful to the public."

I stifled a laugh and studied the snakeskin. "I think she's right, Sean. I don't think this belongs to a garter snake."

"Whatever. It's still not a threat," Sean said. "Just keep your doors and windows closed."

"It could be a threat," I said. "Sometimes people adopt an exotic pet and realize they can't handle it, so they set the animal free. If it's not used to living outside on its own, it could misbehave."

Sean pressed his lips together. "Fine. I'll check out the rest of the neighborhood. Maybe a neighbor knows something."

Eloise angled her head to the left. "Start with Mrs.

Langley next door. She hates me. She probably bought the snake just to release it into my yard and mess with me."

"Why does she hate you?" I asked. I thought of my own family's subtle feud with Mrs. Paulson next door. The elderly woman was too nosy for her own good.

Eloise huffed. "Because she thinks I ruined her beloved azaleas."

"Why would she think that?" I asked.

"Because they died."

I cast a quick glance at Sean. "Did you do something to them?"

She folded her arms. "If vomit has a negative impact on the health of azaleas, then I guess it's possible. I don't see why it wouldn't act as a special fertilizer though. There had to be some nutrients in there."

I frowned. "Why did you barf in her azaleas?"

"It wasn't deliberate," Eloise said. "In my defense, it was dark and I thought I was in my bathroom."

"How drunk were you?" Sean asked.

Eloise wrapped a strand of blond hair around her finger. "On a scale of tipsy to unconscious?" She pondered the question. "I remembered to hold my hair back. I woke up on the lawn, though, so I guess that counts as unconscious."

"Did your neighbor see you there?" I asked.

"Why do you think I woke up? She turned the hose on me."

Oh boy. I could see why their relationship wasn't so neighborly.

"To be fair, she hated me before the azalea incident," Eloise admitted. "She thinks I'm a blight on the neighborhood. She also doesn't like cats, which basically means there's a spot reserved for her in hell." She looked down at the cat. "Isn't that right, Mischief?"

The Siamese cat meowed in response.

"Okay, Deputy Guthrie and I will canvas the neighborhood and let you know if we find anything."

"Do you need a gun?" Eloise asked.

Sean jerked toward her. "You own a gun?"

Eloise blanched. "No. Nope. I wouldn't dream of owning an unlicensed firearm. I'm a responsible, law-abiding citizen."

Sean muttered under his breath, as we left the house and headed next door to Mrs. Langley's house. I stopped to look underneath the dark blue Honda Accord in Mrs. Langley's driveway in case there was a snake lurking.

"The coast is clear," I told Sean.

"You don't have to tell me," he said. "It's not like I care if I see it."

I smiled at him over my shoulder. "Is that why you're sticking so close to me?"

He stopped walking to widen the gap between us. "I'm not."

I made a hissing sound and he scowled. I laughed and stepped onto the porch. The front door was open, so I knocked on the screen door.

"Mrs. Langley?" I called. I peered inside. There was no sign of movement. "Hello, Mrs. Langley?"

"She's probably old," Sean said. "You need to ring the bell." He pressed the button and we heard the shrill sound from outside. "She can't miss that noise, no matter how deaf she is."

When there was no response, I cracked open the screen door and called her name. Still no answer.

"We should go in," I said. Now that I knew it wasn't Charlemagne, all bets were off as to the snake's temperament. There could be an old lady suffering from a snake bite somewhere inside.

Sean's pale, freckled brow lifted. "Why would we do that?"

"The snake might have come here after Eloise scared it away. Or what if she's fallen and can't get up?" There were enough advertisements about that to suggest it actually happened.

"What if she's in the bathtub and naked?" Sean countered.

"Like you don't have firsthand experience with a wrinkled prune," I shot back.

"I don't know what Tanner ever saw in you."

I tensed, not wanting to think about the whole Tanner debacle. "It was high school, Sean. Give it a rest." I held open the screen door. "You can arrest me when I come out if you want, but I'm going in."

"Stop being so dramatic. I'm coming."

I entered the house with Sean right behind me. The small foyer was welcoming, with a painted console table covered in country style knick knacks. A ceramic chicken that looked straight out of a senior citizen's class. A rustic metal pitcher. A wooden sign that spelled 'love' with each letter painted a different muted color. We continued into the kitchen and I noticed a dirty bowl and spoon in the sink. A mug of water sat on the counter next to the stove. There was no sign of a teabag. I placed my hands around the mug. Cold.

"I'll check the bedroom and bathroom to preserve your modesty," I said.

"It's not my modesty I'm worried about," he said. "I'll scope out the living room."

I crept along the hallway, calling her name again. The wall was lined with photographs of family members, including a double frame with an older couple on one side and their younger selves on the other. It was sweet. I filed the idea away for a time when I could display a framed photograph of Sawyer and me, assuming such a day ever came. And if

Grandma hexed us, we could include that photo of our older selves sooner rather than later.

That's looking on the bright side, Eden.

The bathroom was empty. She wasn't in the bedroom either, although there were clean clothes placed neatly on the bed. I checked the other bedrooms before meeting up with Sean in the living room.

"I wonder if she's part of that program where a driver picks her up and brings her to appointments," I said. I knew several senior citizens that took part in the program, like Grandma's friend Shirley. Although, to be honest, Shirley had no trouble driving. She just enjoyed being chauffeured around. She said it made her feel like Joan Collins, whoever that is. It was possible that Mrs. Langley no longer felt comfortable driving but was reluctant to give up her car. I could understand that. The car was probably her last link to complete independence.

"I can check the hospital," Sean said. "Make sure she wasn't brought in."

"Let's check with the other neighbors first," I said. "If she's anything like Aunt Thora, she's probably sitting in someone's kitchen with a cup of tea and a story." Aunt Thora was like me. She sought relationships outside of the family as a way of staying sane.

We left the house and I closed both doors behind me. No need to encourage a burglar with an open door.

"We should divide and conquer," Sean said. "I'll take the houses across the street."

"Okay, make sure to ask about the snake too," I said. "If it's as big as Eloise claims, then they should be on alert, especially if they have small children or pets."

Sean's eyes popped in a comical fashion. "You think a snake could pose a threat to kids?"

"One hundred percent," I said. "Did you never learn about them in school? They can crack open their jaws and…"

He held up a hand. "I don't need nightmares, Fury. Seeing your face this long is enough of a challenge."

I chucked the snakeskin at him. "You'll need to take this to the office." I laughed as he shrank from the flimsy material.

"I don't need it," he said, and I detected a slight whine in his voice. By the gods, I really hoped to get the chief back in working human condition soon. I always knew Sean Guthrie wasn't an adequate substitute and this was proof.

I spun on my heel and jogged to the house on the other side of Mrs. Langley's. All the houses on this street were well-maintained. I could understand why Mrs. Langley was upset about her azaleas. You never want to be the one to bring down the neighborhood. Then again, it seemed that, in this neighborhood, the honor belonged to Eloise Worthington.

I knocked on the door and a middle-aged man answered. He was bald and portly and, judging from his T-shirt and sweatpants, on his way out the door for a workout.

"Can I help you?" he asked, his face tense.

"My name is Agent Fury," I said. "I was checking on Mrs. Langley next door. Her front door was open, but she doesn't appear to be home. Do you happen to know where she is?"

He seemed to relax. "Boy, you had me worried there for a second. It's Monday, so she's probably at her physical therapy session. She has tendonitis in her shoulder."

"Oh, is she unable to drive?" I asked.

"She's had her son drive her ever since the flareup," he said. "Holding the steering wheel aggravates it."

"She told you that?"

He laughed under his breath. "More times than I care to count. She takes prescription strength ibuprofen too. I can also tell you about her reaction to the shingles vaccine." He shook his head. "Spoiler alert: it wasn't good."

I smiled. "Thanks, that's helpful. Mr...?"

"Garrett," he said. "My wife and I have lived next door for about fifteen years, so we know Mrs. Langley and her schedule pretty well."

Better than he'd like, apparently.

"One more question," I said. "Any chance you've seen a large snake in the neighborhood?"

His brow lifted. "Are you serious?"

"Yes, one of your neighbors reported seeing one and I found snakeskin that corroborated her story. If you have any small pets or children, I'd suggest not leaving them outside unattended until the snake's been caught."

Mr. Garrett nodded profusely. "I'll be sure to keep our cats inside. My wife would die if anything happened to them."

"Deputy Guthrie is spreading the word with your other neighbors," I said.

"I can post to our neighborhood Facebook page," he said. "That way everyone sees the alert."

"Thanks, that would be helpful." I started to leave.

"If you don't mind my asking," Mr. Garrett began, "why is a federal agent checking on Mrs. Langley? Is she in some kind of trouble?" Worry lines formed between his eyebrows.

"No, not at all. I was actually dealing with Eloise on the corner."

The lines disappeared. "Ah, that makes more sense."

I smiled. "She's a handful, I take it."

"She's something," Mr. Garret said vaguely, but the implication was clear.

I tilted my head toward the driveway. "For what it's worth, your azaleas are in good shape."

"Yeah, as long as Eloise doesn't go on any more benders, we expect to keep them that way."

I left the Garrets' house and finished talking to neighbors on my side of the street. Of the people currently home, no one had seen a snake. Sean and I reconvened in front of Eloise's house. I told him about Mrs. Langley's appointment and that I'd seen no further evidence of the snake.

"I found more snakeskin in the yard directly across the street." He pointed to the house on the corner opposite where we were standing. "No snake though."

"I guess you should call Animal Control now that I know it isn't Charlemagne," I said. "People will start to get anxious now that they know it's out there. They'll feel better if they see someone actively pursuing it."

"Yeah, I don't want any more phone calls to deal with." He dragged a hand through his red hair. "How long did you say until the chief's better?"

I felt a rush of tenderness for the poor chief. "Not soon enough."

CHAPTER FIVE

AFTER SEAN RETURNED me to my car in front of the diner, I Googled 'food for foxes' and was pleased to see cheese on the list of foods that they eat. That was easy. Unsurprisingly, I opted to bypass raw meat. I ran into the nearest store and contemplated the overwhelming choices.

"Hello, Eden," the owner said. As a descendant of Francis Worland, one of the Puritan settlers, Joan Worland had owned and operated Brie-licious since before I was born. She was at least seventy years old, but with her relatively smooth skin and ash blond hair, she didn't look a day over fifty. If I didn't know for certain that she was human, I'd swear she was a vampire.

"How are you, Joan?"

"I'd heard you moved back to town," the older woman said. "City life didn't agree with you, I suppose."

"Something like that." I hated having to explain my reasons for returning to Chipping Cheddar, especially because there was no way to do it honestly. "The agency transferred me to another division."

She frowned. "Yes, I heard. It's money laundering?"

"No, cyber crime. Online fraud."

Joan shook her head. "I don't know much about that. I stay off the internet. Too much fake news circulating. I rely on *The Buttermilk Bugle* and that's about it." She perked up. "Say, isn't your friend Clara a reporter there? So nice to see you kids grown up and doing important work. Cheese is all I've ever known." She placed a palm flat on the counter, seemingly lost in thought. "That's what happens when you take over a family business."

"Didn't you get a choice?"

Joan blew a raspberry. "It was take over or sell the business. My grandfather always said cheesemaking's in our blood. He would've climbed out of his grave like one of those zombies in the movies and given me an earful if I'd have let the shop fall into someone else's hands."

I laughed. "If the only thing zombies did was lecture people about their poor life choices, there'd be far fewer horror movies."

"Well, you didn't venture in here to catch up on my life story," Joan said. "What brings you in? Your Aunt Thora was in here just yesterday, so I can't imagine you're out of cheddar already."

I surveyed the variety of cheeses. "This might seem like an odd question, but there's a fox that's been visiting my friend's garden and we want to feed him. Apparently, foxes like cheese, so what do you think? Asiago is probably too nutty for him, right? Is American too bland?"

Joan chuckled. "Pair the American with a nice wine and you're golden."

A blush rose to my cheeks. "I told you it was an odd question."

"That's quite a lot of thought you're putting into fox food. Are you planning to serve crackers with it? I have a nice selection of those too."

"Just cheese, thanks." I examined a block of Beaufort. Too expensive. "Chevaigne will work."

"No problem. Anything else?"

"As a matter of fact there is." I pulled out my wallet as she rang up the order. "Do you know anything about a secret society for Puritan descendants?"

Joan's hand hovered over the register. "What makes you ask about that?"

I gave her a twenty-dollar bill. "Clara's writing an article about them for the paper and I thought you might be a good source for her."

Joan's mouth tightened as she handed over my change. "It's a secret society, Eden. Why would anyone talk to a newspaper reporter about it?"

"You could be anonymous," I said. "I mean, why does the town need a secret society anyway? What purpose does it serve?"

Joan tapped her rounded fingernails on the counter. "Never you mind, Eden Fury. You and Clara don't have roots as deep as some folks here, so you wouldn't understand."

And there it was. The suppressed air of superiority. "Sometimes roots get twisted and damage the trees they're meant to support," I said.

"I'd advise Clara not to go poking around in things that aren't her business."

"She's a reporter," I said. "It's in the job description." What was so sacred that Joan felt the need to turn hostile at the mere mention of the club?

Joan's hand flicked out and she handed me the bag of cheese. "Hope the fox enjoys his treat. Seems a bit decadent to me, but then again, your family's always bordered on the strange side."

My face hardened. "You know, Joan, there are plenty of

cheese shops in town. My family doesn't need to support this one."

Joan flashed a fake smile. "Suit yourself."

I left Brie-licious in a huff. Joan's reaction was exactly why I disliked the idea of a secret club for descendants. It seemed like an excuse to establish an unnecessary pecking order in town. Why jockey for position? Just be neighborly.

I drove to the chief's house to check on him. I didn't like the idea of leaving him alone all day. He had to be scared.

I parked on a side street so that no one saw my car and hurried to the back door. I'd left it unlocked so that I could slip in unnoticed.

"Sawyer," I called, opening the door. "It's me."

The house was quiet. I went to the kitchen first and placed the bag of cheese on the counter before continuing to the bedroom. The food and water that I'd left for him were empty, so that was a good sign. I worried that he'd be too upset to eat and starve himself. I continued to the master bedroom. The comforter was askew and the sheets were tangled, but the fox was nowhere to be found. Uh oh. He couldn't possibly have gotten out, could he?

"Sawyer?" I raced through the house, checking for anywhere a fox could have escaped. There were no open doors or windows. When I turned to check the backyard, I spotted it. The back door had a cat flap. It was white and blended in with the rest of the door, so I hadn't noticed it before. The previous homeowner must've had a cat or a small dog.

"Gods above," I hissed. Why would he leave? Was he thinking like a chief or a fox?

I ran outside and scoured the backyard. What if he came into contact with the giant snake? My heart began to pound as I pictured a standoff between them. I had to find him. I was careful not to yell too loudly and alert the neighbors.

They couldn't know I was there and they certainly couldn't know that the chief of police had been turned into a fox.

I covered every blade of grass, looking for any evidence that pointed to which direction he went. I found nothing, not even trampled flowers. I was going to have to enlist the aid of my favorite wizard. I pulled out my phone and called Neville.

"I was wondering where you were," he said, by way of greeting. "I have Achilles with me at the office and he's already chewed two wires and your mousepad."

"My mousepad?" I echoed. "How did he get that?"

"I might have tossed it to him like a Frisbee when he started sniffing around my backpack."

I couldn't be annoyed with Neville. After all, he was doing me a favor that was outside the scope of his FBM duties. Nowhere in the manual did it mention dogsitting for members of law enforcement turned into foxes.

"I've been delayed," I said. "I have a situation."

"Oh? Anything I can assist with?"

"That's why I'm calling," I said. "The chief is missing and I need to find him."

"Have you tried calling him?" Neville asked. "Not on the phone, of course. I recognize the inadequacy of that suggestion when the chief currently lacks opposable thumbs."

I sighed. "Telling me to yell his name is the equivalent of telling me to turn my computer off and on when I have a problem."

He chuckled. "I do instruct you to try that more often than not."

I felt the tension creeping into my shoulders, so I stretched my neck from side to side. "I left him at his house last night, which I now realize was a big mistake, and he's missing. He snuck out through the cat flap."

"Dearie me."

"Exactly. So, I need a little wizard help in tracking him.

There's also a supersized snake on the loose and I'd rather the two of them not square off."

Neville lit up. "It could be like Godzilla versus Mother."

"No, it really couldn't." I gave him the chief's address and hung up. In addition to my pounding heart, my palms were now sweaty. The more I thought about poor Sawyer trapped in animal form, the more worried I became. He could get hit by a car, or drown in the river, or be lost in the woods forever. Gods have mercy, now I sounded like my cousin Julie. She was forever fretting about Meg dying in a ditch.

I returned to the house to get a strand of Sawyer's hair for the spell. Luckily, his hair was thick and I was able to snag a few pieces from his brush. I waited outside, pacing the length of the backyard to keep my body occupied. Anything to curb my rising anxiety. I sagged with relief when Neville appeared.

"What took you so long?" I asked.

"What do you think? I had to take Achilles for a quick walk and then gather supplies." He set his backpack on the ground. "I expect you need me to do a locator spell."

I nodded. "I have strands of his hair."

"Perfect." He held out his hand and I gave him the hair. As he prepared his magic circle, he glanced up at me. "Do you know yet how this happened?"

"I have no idea," I said. "One minute we were on a date, having a wonderful time, and the next minute I was kissing a pointed snout." I hadn't told him that part when I'd dropped off Achilles. It seemed too personal.

"Do you think it's your family?"

"That was my first thought, but I didn't see any evidence of their involvement. As far as I know, they're still clueless about us." I observed Neville as he lit a candle and began the incantation. I gave him space to work, not wanting to mess up the spell. Time was of the essence.

Neville tipped back his head to look at me. "He's near water."

"Gee, that's super helpful when we're adjacent to the bay *and* the river. Right up there with telling me that Mount Everest is located in the Himalayas."

Neville tugged his ear. "He's near the mound."

Of course. He'd been impacted by something supernatural, so naturally he'd be drawn to the area where the portal and the vortex were located. His body was probably more in tune with magical energy than his mind was.

"Let's go," I said.

Neville blew out the candle and swept the items into his backpack. "Do you want me to drive?"

"We'll drive separately in case we need to split up," I said. "Did you leave Achilles at the office?"

"I dropped him off next door," he said. "Paige is looking after him."

"You didn't tell her anything, did you?"

He pulled a face. "Do I look like an amateur to you?"

I shrugged. "Sometimes?"

He huffed. "I told her that the chief was too sick to look after the poor pup and we were taking turns but had an emergency."

"Good thinking."

We parted ways on the sidewalk by the house and I slipped into my car before anyone spotted me. I pressed the pedal to the floor, knowing that there was little chance of a speeding ticket with Deputy Guthrie filling in for the chief. He was probably in the office right now, sobbing into a corned beef sandwich.

I snagged a parking spot near Davenport Park and hit the brakes, rocking back and forth from the sudden stop. I bolted from the car and began my frantic search. There were people in the park with their dogs, so I couldn't call his name without raising suspicion.

Neville appeared beside me. "I'll check the vortex." A vortex is a place where multiple ley lines converge and powerful energy can be harnessed and we had our very own energy center right in Chipping Cheddar.

"Then I'll check the portal." I'd recently shown the portal to the chief after revealing the truth about the supernatural world to him. Maybe he'd gone there in search of answers.

To garden-variety humans, the mound is simply a hillside near the river and the Chesapeake Bay. Little do they know that a dormant portal to Otherworld is located inside. A portal that I routinely check to make sure that it's still dormant and that no demons or other supernaturals have breached the border.

I entered the hillside and let my eyesight adjust to the darkness. "Sawyer?" The small fox was curled up in a corner near the portal. I ran to him and dropped to my knees. "Are you okay?"

The fox looked at me with soulful eyes. He opened his mouth as if to speak but no sound came out.

Neville rushed inside. "He wasn't at the vortex." He halted in his tracks when he saw me on the ground with the fox. "You're sure that's him and not some random fox from the woods?"

"What are the odds that a random fox came to check out the portal?" I demanded.

"Stranger things have happened," Neville argued.

I stroked the fox's head. "It's him. I can tell." I felt his presence in there. The fox form was merely a shell that housed the real Sawyer.

"How's the portal?" Neville asked.

"Still dormant," I said. I faced the fox. "I'm not taking any more chances. You're coming home with me."

"Isn't that a different kind of risk?" Neville asked.

"I'll hide him in the attic. There's no reason for my family to look there. Besides, if they do find him, they'll think I've adopted a fox. It won't be the first time I've come home with a rescue animal. They won't suspect it's the chief."

"And what about Achilles?"

"Will you keep looking after him?" I asked. "I know it's no small request…"

"I'll do it," Neville said, more quickly than I expected.

"Great."

"Do you know how many women spoke to me today?" he asked. "Three. All because I was walking the dog. The pug is magical."

"Maybe you should ask one of them out," I said. "Your reward for doing a good deed."

Neville puffed out his chest. "Maybe I will." He paused. "If I manage to make eye contact next time. I haven't been able to do it thus far."

Poor Neville. He really needed a dating coach, but there was no time to ponder that right now. I gathered the fox in my arms and headed for my car.

"Best of luck, Agent Fury," Neville called.

"Thanks, Neville." Because I was definitely going to need it.

CHAPTER SIX

I'D BARELY MADE it into the attic with the fox when I heard my mother's voice reverberating downstairs. I couldn't make out the words. I sat on the mattress and cradled Sawyer on my lap. "When I've pictured you between my legs, this isn't exactly what I had in mind."

The fox observed me silently. Even without their brilliant sea-green color, his eyes were mesmerizing. I realized that I still felt drawn to him, despite his fox form. Was this what people meant when they talked about soulmates? That no matter what form someone inhabited, if he was your soulmate, you'd still recognize him as yours? My neck warmed when I realized I was thinking about Sawyer as my soulmate. It was way too early in the relationship for that kind of thought—wasn't it?

"I'm so sorry this happened to you," I said. I buried my face in his thick coat. "I promise to make it right."

The fox nuzzled me and I started to relax. I felt guilty for what happened, even though I had no idea whether the change was related to me.

"I bought you cheese, but I left it at your house," I said. "I know there's good cheddar here, so I can bring you some of that if you're hungry."

The fox swished his tail.

"If you hear me talking to someone, it's Alice Wentworth," I continued. "She's a ghost that lives here. This farmhouse was part of her family farm back in the day. She's very nice."

The fox cocked his head, listening.

"I'm kind of embarrassed that you have to see this place," I said. "It's not very grownup to live on a mattress in the attic of your childhood home. The good news is that the barn will be finished soon and then I'll have my own place." I sighed deeply and stroked his fur, withholding the remainder of my thoughts—that the barn was still uncomfortably close to my family and the whole thing was probably a mistake. The chief had enough to handle right now without my own fears and insecurities.

As though sensing my distress, the fox placed a paw on my arm. Even as a woodland animal, he was a sensitive and compassionate being. Where did this miracle man come from?

"You left Iowa, a place you seem to like," I said. "What made you do that? I wanted to get as far away from here as possible." I settled against the pillow and the fox wedged in beside me. "My dream was to work for the FBI. Do you have any idea what it's like to work hard for something and finally get it, only to have it snatched away?"

We sat in silence for a moment, mainly because the fox couldn't talk and I felt awkward holding a one-sided conversation.

"I feel like I bring trouble wherever I go because of my true nature," I said. "If I were a regular human like you, everything would be so much easier."

Alice materialized in the attic, causing me to jump. "You'd better come, Eden. Your mother is on a rampage."

My heart skipped a beat. "Why?"

"You'll have to see for yourself to understand."

That didn't bode well. "Am I a target?" That was a question Anton and I used to ask each other often as teenagers. It meant the difference between staying out later or going home.

"I don't think so, but she's angry enough that anyone is fair game right now."

Terrific. I chose the ideal home to sneak in my human-turned-fox boyfriend. I got off the mattress and shook a finger at him. "Stay here and under no circumstances do you come downstairs. Do you understand?"

The fox seemed to nod.

"How sweet," Alice said, admiring the fox. "He wears that fur well, don't you think?"

"I don't care if he wears it well," I said. "I want it off him."

"I preferred men without beards too," Alice said, "but we don't always get to choose the fashion of our time."

I fled the attic to see what my mother was angry about. As I hurried to the kitchen, I nearly collided with an old woman. At first I thought Aunt Thora had invited a friend over. The woman wasn't tall enough to be Shirley, Grandma's human friend.

"Excuse me," I said, and then froze. "Mom?"

The woman's skin had more wrinkles than Anton's shirt after a nap in the car. Her hunched shoulders made her appear a couple inches shorter than her usual height. There was no mistaking the eyes though. Over the past twenty-six years, I'd seen them express every emotion, including the one they displayed right now.

Pure, unadulterated rage.

"Your grandmother thought it would be hilarious to hex me before my date tonight," she seethed. Her voice trembled slightly in the way that elderly vocal cords were wont to do.

Grandma and Aunt Thora sat at the table. Grandma nibbled on a cookie, maintaining a neutral expression. Her phone rested in front of her.

"Why did you hex her with a premature aging spell?" I asked.

Grandma kept chewing. "I admit nothing."

My mother marched to the table. "You undo this hex right now."

Grandma picked up her phone and tapped the screen. "I'm afraid I'm fully booked today. Try again tomorrow."

My mother's familiar eyes flashed with anger. "This means war."

I shook my head at Grandma. "Why didn't you just kill her? That would've been kinder than making her old." My mother's vanity couldn't handle the sudden change.

"Because Thora made that murder jar," Grandma said.

"What's a murder jar?" I asked, though I was sure I'd regret the question.

Grandma pointed behind me to a glass jar with a yellow ribbon tied around the mouth. "That."

"How is that a murder jar?"

"It's like a swear jar," Aunt Thora said. "Every time they kill each other, they have to put money in the jar. I figure it will pay for Olivia's college tuition. Maybe even Ryan's."

"Grandma's too cheap," I said, nodding my approval. "It's a useful deterrent." Hence the premature aging spell on my mother. "Why does it have a yellow ribbon?"

"Because yellow is my favorite color," Aunt Thora said.

I should have known.

My mother's arthritic fingers worked hard to roll up her sleeves. There was a murderous glint in her eye. "I have money stocked away. I can afford the jar."

Aunt Thora sprang to her feet. "Now, Beatrice. Let's not be hasty."

"What did you do to Grandma to deserve this?" I asked.

My mother's nostrils flared. "I did nothing to deserve this. No one deserves to be old before their time. It's cruel and inhumane."

"Ha!" Grandma said, without looking up from her phone. "Oh, it's my lucky day. I've been trying to catch this little guy for ages. He sparkles."

"Your lucky day, is it?" my mother said through gritted teeth.

"Luckier than yours," Grandma shot back.

"Mom, what did you do?" I insisted. There was no way Grandma would go this far without provocation.

"I did the laundry," my mother said. "That's the crime I'm guilty of."

"You washed a tissue in with my clothes," Grandma said. "I had to pluck little pieces of snotty white tissue off my good black slacks."

"Nobody says slacks anymore," my mother said.

"Nobody says fill me up, buttercup anymore either, yet I've heard you say that to more than one date this decade." Grandma glared at my mother.

"Can we stay focused?" I asked. "How do you even know the tissue is her fault? Maybe someone else left the tissue in a pocket. Just because Mom did the laundry doesn't mean she left it in there."

Grandma leveled me with a look. "Look at you. One shiny badge and suddenly you're sticking your nose in all sorts of places it doesn't belong."

My confidence wobbled slightly. I recognized that glint in her eye. She would be more than happy to strike me with an aging hex and I couldn't afford to fight that battle with the chief in a precarious situation.

"Can you please undo the hex, Grandma?" I asked. "Mom has a date tonight with a human. He can't see her like this."

Grandma shrugged. "She should try one of those wrinkle creams she's so fond of." She shot a dark look at my mother. "And apply it liberally."

Hostility rolled off my mother in waves and I blocked her warpath with a well-placed arm. "Grandma, you know that regular wrinkle cream won't do anything for this."

Grandma fixated on her phone. "Then I suppose she'll have to cancel until the wrinkles fade. Could take weeks."

"Or you can undo the spell before I undo you," my mother snarled.

I held her back, hoping that my fury strength wouldn't be required. I shot Aunt Thora a helpless look. I was going to need assistance.

"Ladies, if you can't work this out, I'm going to lock you in a room together," Aunt Thora warned.

Grandma appeared unconcerned. "Like your measly magic could keep us contained."

"Maybe hers can't, but mine can," I said. Gods, why did I let myself get dragged into this now? I had far more important things to do.

My mother gave me an anxious look and took a step backward, out of my reach.

Grandma laughed. "Yours only can if you siphon it from one of us. Good luck doing that to me. You'll be crying blood tears."

"Is that a spell?" Aunt Thora asked.

"No, it's from the urban dictionary," Grandma said. "It means I will aggressively hurt her."

Yeah, blood tears about summed it up. I couldn't back down now though. If I showed weakness, I was going to end up buried in the garden and I couldn't afford that kind of delay.

"I have other powers, Grandma," I said. "I don't need to siphon anything to kick your black magic butt."

Grandma's expression hardened. "Be careful or I'm going to curse you like Gautama cursed Indra."

"With a thousand eyes on my body?" I asked.

"No, they were originally a thousand marks of vaginas," Grandma said. "And if you really piss me off, they'll all get their periods at the same time."

Aunt Thora slid back her chair and stood. "I think that's my cue to leave."

"Go on then," Grandma said. "Go to the lighthouse and consort with that human companion of yours."

"If you weren't so old already, I'd hex you with an aging spell and see how you like it." Aunt Thora put her teacup and saucer in the sink before striding from the room.

"You are going to rue the day you decided to hex me, Esther Pritchard." My mother stomped her foot and whimpered. "Ouch. My brittle bones can't handle that much impact."

"Worth it," Grandma said, and returned her attention to Little Critters on her phone.

I wasn't going to get anywhere right now. Grandma was clearly set on punishing my mother no matter the consequences. I turned to face my mother.

"Pro tip: the ice cream shop hosts senior Sundays," I said. "Lots of guys your age."

"They're not my age." She tried to stomp her foot again but found she couldn't lift her leg high enough for impact. She whirled around and shuffled to her bedroom, whimpering. The bedroom door slammed and I winced at the sound. It reminded me of the fights my parents used to have. For a few seconds, I was six years old and ready to walk on eggshells for the rest of the day.

I drew a deep, calming breath and approached the table. "Grandma, I really don't think the punishment fits the crime. So you had to pick off pieces of tissue. Big deal. I bet you could've conjured a spell to remove the mess instead of kicking up a fuss."

Grandma tapped her phone screen repeatedly. "She was already on my bad side. The laundry was the last straw."

"Okay, fine. Have your fun, but please don't let it last too long. What if she actually gets hurt in this condition? She could break a hip."

Grandma's lips melted into a smile that reminded me of the Grinch. "She could, couldn't she?"

I groaned. "I wasn't trying to give you ideas. Please don't break her hip. We'll be waiting on her hand and foot for months. We won't survive."

"Good point." Grandma didn't make eye contact. "I won't let her twist in the wind too long."

"Thank you." I needed some air after that heated standoff. I decided to put a little distance between my bickering family members and me—five hundred yards, to be exact. I opened the back door to my father's house that he shared with my stepmom, Sally, the most elegant vampire in Chipping Cheddar by a mile. My father met her on a business trip to Otherworld and never looked back. They were much more suited to each other than my mother and father were. There was no door slamming. No children caught in the middle. No yelling. Well, that wasn't entirely accurate. My father's natural volume was set to Extremely Loud and Uncomfortably Close, even when he was engaged in idle chitchat.

"Eden, what a nice surprise." Sally was bent over the countertop in the kitchen, scrubbing vigorously with a sponge. Did I mention the vampire also has OCD?

"What happened?" I asked.

Sally stopped scrubbing and set the sponge on the edge of the sink. "Nothing major. There's a fleck of grease that's being stubborn. You know I can't abide a filthy kitchen."

I loved that a single fleck of grease translated to 'filthy' in the vampire's mind. She would die all over again if she saw the state of the attic. My clothes were strewn across the top of cardboard boxes.

"Can I get you a snack, darling?" Sally asked. "I have homemade baclava." She smiled, showing her fangs. "Your father's special request."

"No, thanks. I'm good." I scanned the living room. "Is he around?"

"He's around," a voice bellowed. Stanley Fury rounded the corner, carrying a set of golf clubs. "He's getting ready to hit the green, though."

"I won't be long," I said. "I just need to ask a question."

My father set down the bag and regarded me. "Me first. Are you doing those stretches I told you to do?"

I resisted the urge to roll my eyes. "Yes, Dad," I lied.

"I don't think you are." He circled me. "I can tell by how round your shoulders are. Suck in a breath and tighten your diaphragm."

It was easier to comply than to argue, especially when I wanted him to answer my question. I inhaled deeply and pressed my palm flat against my abdomen. "Better?"

"Do you feel the difference?" my father asked. "You should. You walk around like Quasimodo for too long and you'll end up with osteoporosis."

"That's not how osteoporosis works, Dad. It's a calcium or vitamin D deficiency." It could also be the result of hormonal changes, but there was no way I was saying the word 'hormones' to my father. We didn't have that type of relationship.

He pointed a finger at me. "Are you trying to tell me I'm wrong?"

"Relax, Stanley," Sally said. "Have a snack. Your blood sugar is probably low."

My mother's door slam must have triggered some kind

61

of PTSD because now I was seven years old, listening at my bedroom door as my parents fought. I don't even remember the substantive part of the argument, only that each one wanted to be right more than they wanted to be married. Stanley and Beatrice Fury were never wrong, which made arguments impossible to resolve. Major or minor, it didn't matter. They were always right and they never apologized.

"Stanley, she looks nothing like Quasimodo," Sally said. "Doesn't he have an eye patch?"

"He has a giant wart that covers his left eye," I said, my voice even.

"Stay on your mother's good side or you'll have one of those too," my father said.

I debated whether to tell him about her current condition but decided against it. It was always best to err on the side of discretion when it came to my parents' current affairs. If I told my father, then my mother would accuse me of 'choosing sides.'

"Clasp your hands behind your back and open up that chest area," my father urged. "That's where your problem is. Those muscles shorten up and pull the rest of you forward." He walked into the kitchen and took a glass from the cabinet.

I performed the stretch while I asked my question because it was the fastest way out of here. "Have you ever exacted revenge by turning your target into an animal?"

My father filled the glass with water and drank. He smacked his lips together once he finished. "That's pretty specific. Do you have a job you want me to handle? Who is it —that deputy you can't stand? I can turn him into a weasel for you." He refilled the glass. "No, something better that goes with red hair. A fox?"

I waved my arms in a panic. "No foxes. And it's not about Deputy Guthrie," I said. As much as it pained me to admit it, the town desperately needed him in his human form right now.

Sally found a new flaw on the counter to obsess over. She picked up the sponge and began a fresh round of intense rubbing. "Is it Tanner Hughes? He could definitely stand to spend some time in weasel form. I know he still gives you a hard time when he sees you."

"How do you know that?" I hated being the object of any gossip in town, although I knew it was all but impossible to prevent.

"I've been within earshot on occasion when you've run into him."

Sally's enchanted vampire hearing allowed her to excel in eavesdropping. Lucky for Chipping Cheddar that she wasn't a huge gossip.

"It's not Tanner," I said. "I don't want to reap vengeance on anyone. You know how I feel about it."

My father snorted. "Puritan."

I glared at him. "Hypothetically, if someone has been turned into an animal, is there any chance it's the work of a vengeance demon?"

"Is this hypothetical transformation taking place in Chipping Cheddar?" he asked.

"Yes."

"Then it's not a vengeance demon," he said firmly. "Nobody comes in or out of here without my knowledge." He paused. "And my blessing."

Sally looped her arm through his. "He's like the Godfather of vengeance demons. The others wouldn't want to mess with him."

"And no one's come to town recently?" I asked. For all I knew, Chief Fox had unwittingly made enemies in Iowa with connections to the supernatural world.

"Nope," my father said. "Whatever's going on, it's not due

to a vengeance demon."

On the one hand, his certainty was a relief. On the other hand, I still had no idea how or why this happened to the chief.

"Who's been turned into an animal?" my father asked. "Anyone I know?"

"It's hypothetical, remember?" I said with a pointed look. "This conversation is confidential."

My father waved me off. "Yeah, yeah. I'll keep your official FBM secrets."

"Thanks, Dad." I started toward the door.

"Where are you going?" my father asked. His tone was so demanding—like I was attempting to walk out of prison before my official release date.

"There's someone in town I have to see," I said. Now that I'd ruled out my family and a vengeance demon, I had another cauldron to stir.

"Are you driving?" he asked.

"That's the plan." The wings were only for emergency purposes.

"Make sure you go to the gas station on Asiago," he said. "The one on Mozzarella Street is up two cents a gallon. It's highway robbery."

"Technically, it's not a highway, Stanley," Sally said.

Although Asiago was out of my way and I didn't need to fill up my tank, a quick escape was better than an argument. "Okay. Thanks." I opened the back door.

"And stand up straight," he bellowed. "Any further forward and you'll end up in a somersault. You don't need a head injury."

In an exaggerated motion, I shoved my shoulders back so far that I was sure my shoulder blades were touching. As I closed the door behind me, I heard my father say, "That's much better."

CHAPTER SEVEN

I breezed into Magic Beans, the new coffee shop in town, and greeted its owner. "Hey, Corinne."

The witch stood behind the counter with her back to the room while a barista prepared coffee for customers. Business had to be doing well to justify hiring an employee. I was pleased for her.

Corinne turned and smiled. "How's it going, Eden?" As delicious as the coffee was, that wasn't the reason I was here. Corinne happened to be a talented witch and a talented witch was exactly what I needed right now. Our families aren't what you'd call friendly, although I serve on the supernatural council with Adele, Corinne's grandmother. The legacy of the LeRoux witches extends back to New Orleans. They don't practice the same kind of magic as my family members, which was the main reason I decided to come to Corinne for help. I never want to give my family an excuse to practice black magic. Thankfully, Corinne and I seemed to be breaking the cycle of insults and mutual dislike and were developing—dare I say it—an actual friendship.

I leaned against the counter. "Got a minute?"

She seemed to understand that the 'minute' involved a confidential supernatural topic because she wiped her hands on her apron and stepped out from behind the counter. "There's a quiet table over here."

I followed Corinne to a table by the window. "I have a situation and could use your help," I said.

She threaded her fingers together on the table. "Well, that's cutting to the chase."

I glanced toward the counter. "I can see you're busy and I don't want to interrupt your work here."

Corinne fixed her dark eyes on me. "If you're here asking for my help, then it's more serious than how quickly my customers get their hit of caffeine."

"It is. It's about the chief."

Corinne raised her brow. "What's wrong?" She and Chief Fox had dated very briefly and I knew she'd be concerned enough to help. That was another reason I opted to come straight to her and not her grandmother. I certainly wasn't going to start with Rosalie by choice. Corinne's mother was my least favorite LeRoux. When it came to mothers, I almost felt as sorry for Corinne as I did for myself.

"He's not himself," I said. I didn't know why I was finding it so hard to say the words. If I had to guess, I would say that I was uncomfortable coming to someone for help, especially a LeRoux witch. When you'd spent your entire childhood shielding yourself from evil and negativity, it wasn't easy to poke a hand through the protective bubble so that someone else could take it.

"Eden, you're scaring me." Corinne tugged her phone out of her pocket. "I'm going to call him right now."

"The chief can't answer his phone."

"Has he left it somewhere?"

"No, he's left his hands somewhere." I squeezed my eyes closed. Okay, that sounded awful. "I mean he doesn't have his hands at the moment." Not much better. I blew out a frustrated breath. "He's a fox."

"I hardly see what his looks have to do with anything," Corinne said.

I lowered my voice. "No, I mean he is an actual fox. Someone has cast a spell on him or something."

Corinne gasped and covered her mouth. "What? How?"

"I don't know. It just happened." I didn't want to get into detail and say too much. Although Corinne was aware that the chief and I were interested in each other, I didn't want to divulge any more information. I trusted Corinne to keep our secret. I did not, however, trust Rosalie. The witch would use it as an opportunity to irritate my family and I couldn't allow the chief to get caught in a war between two covens.

Corinne tapped her black-painted fingernails on the table. "And you want us to see if we can reverse the spell?"

I nodded. "Deputy Guthrie is in charge right now, and I think we can both agree that the sooner the chief is back in human form, the better."

"Where is he now?"

"Probably sliding across the floor in the chief's office in his underwear singing *Old Time Rock & Roll*."

Corinne pressed a hand to her forehead. "Not Guthrie. The chief."

"Oh, he's in my attic," I said. "I didn't want to leave him home alone. It's too risky."

"And what about Achilles?"

It made me happy that Corinne showed concern for the dog. I knew she was good people. "He's safe too."

Corinne's gaze darted to the customers at her counter. I could see her assessing the options. "Let me text my family. Can you come to the old mill with the chief in half an hour?"

"Absolutely. Thank you so much."

Corinne reached forward and clasped my hands in hers.

Although my skin always looked pale, next to Corinne's dark skin I looked more translucent than Alice.

"I'm so glad you came to me for help," Corinne said. "No matter how our families behave, I think it's important to rely on each other, especially in a small town like this one."

I knew what she meant. We supernaturals had to stick together in the human world. I didn't disagree, as much as I'd tried to distance myself from my supernatural nature in the past. I never imagined myself working for the Federal Bureau of Magic. I'd wanted a normal life, one without magical influences or my family. One that didn't involve my fury powers. Unfortunately, fate had other plans. Occasionally, I wondered what my life would be like if I hadn't siphoned a vampire's power and tried to bite Fergus, my FBI partner. I wouldn't have returned to Chipping Cheddar and my old life. I'd be in San Francisco, thousands of miles from my family, enjoying excellent Chinese food and a view of the Golden Gate Bridge. On the other hand, if I'd stayed, I wouldn't have met Chief Fox. It was hard to imagine that now.

I pushed back my chair. "Can we keep this between us? I don't want people to panic."

"I take it your family doesn't know," she said.

I shook my head. "And I'd like to keep it that way. I don't need their messy wand prints all over this."

"Understood."

"See you in thirty," I said.

I exited the coffee shop and sped home to retrieve the fox. I turned on Munster Lane, hoping to avoid any family members. My goal was to sneak in and out without interference. As I reached the end of the cul-de-sac, I noticed John Maclaren's truck parked in front of the house. The carpenter had been working on the barn renovations so that I would finally have a place of my own. The mattress in the attic was wearing thin in more ways than one.

The driver's side door opened and I realized that he'd only just arrived. I pulled into the driveway and jumped out to intercept him.

"Hey, John."

He held up his toolbox. "Not to worry. I'm getting to work. See?"

"I'm not worried. I know you've suffered a few setbacks." Some magical. Some not.

"I'm sorry it's taking me so long," he said. "I know you must be anxious to move into your own space."

"You have no idea," I said.

"If it's any consolation, I could be finished as early as the end of this week."

I bit my lip. "Please do not get my hopes up with a statement like that. I'm going to pretend you didn't tell me."

John patted my shoulder. "It can't be that bad living in a nice farmhouse like this one. The Wentworths knew what they were doing when they built this place."

"It's not the building that's suffocating me."

He chuckled. "Feel free to hang out with me in the barn if you want to vent."

I smiled. "As much as I'd love to take any opportunity to complain about my family, I have work to do."

"If you love what you do, you never work a day in your life," John said. He only came to that revelation after he'd won the lottery thanks to a wish-granting demon.

"I don't know," I said. "I love apprehending bad guys, but it still feels like work."

"Suit yourself." He ambled around the side of the house and disappeared.

I bolted into the house and nearly tripped over Princess Buttercup. The hellhound was sprawled across the floor on the way to the attic. I realized she was monopolizing a patch of sunlight that was shining through the window.

"John's here," I told her. "Want to go outside?"

She leaped to her feet and panted, so I went to the back door and opened it. I made sure the coast was clear in the house before running upstairs to grab the fox. He was asleep on my pillow, which would have been adorable if I weren't so panicked about sneaking him out. It occurred to me that I should have brought the invisibility locket that Neville had made for me.

"Hey, buddy," I whispered. "Time to take a little trip." I scooped him into my arms and crept downstairs, listening for any sounds of family members. So far, so good.

"Eden, is that you?"

Merciful gods. Grandma was lurking somewhere. I'd hoped she was walking around town playing Little Critters.

"Eden?" she called again. "Is that you?"

"No," I yelled. I ran from the house like it was on fire and cradled the fox against my chest. To his credit, he remained perfectly still and quiet. He probably sensed my distress. I slid into the car and dumped him on the passenger seat. I didn't wait to buckle myself in before setting off. A quick glance told me that Grandma was on the front porch with her hands on her hips.

I hit the gas pedal and didn't slow down until I reached the stop sign, where I paused to click my seatbelt. The fox placed a paw on my arm and I realized he was looking for reassurance.

"It's going to be okay," I said. "I'm taking you to the LeRoux witches to see if they can undo whatever's been done to you."

The fox sat straight in his seat and I buckled him in. Then I cracked open the window for fresh air. The attic had to be stuffy for him. Whether in fox form or human form, he was accustomed to spending a lot of time outdoors.

"Any opinion on music?" I asked. I flicked on the radio and *Shake It Off* blasted through the speakers. The fox wasted no time in stretching his seatbelt so that he could tap the button with his paw and change the channel. I suppressed a laugh. Even in fox form, he wasn't going to resign himself to listening to Taylor Swift.

The old mill was officially known as Brie Mill. It was situated beside the disused canal that ran alongside the Susquehanna River. Once owned by the de Valettes, one of the few French families in Chipping Cheddar, Brie Mill flourished during the nineteenth century. The four-story tall building had served as a merchant mill where wheat was ground into flour and sold as far as the Caribbean. According to Alice, the mill had acted as a commercial center in its prime. Locals would flock here to trade goods and services. Whereas the market downtown primarily catered to cheesemakers, the mill served a broader purpose. For the LeRoux witches, I suspected that purpose was to harness the elemental energy that emanated from the moving water.

Sure enough, when I arrived with the fox, the trio of witches were preparing their magic circle on the land in front of the rotating wheel. Adele was the first one to spot me. Wearing a pearl necklace, a ruffled blouse, and a long skirt that swirled around her ankles, the older witch exuded grace and style. She greeted me with a kiss on each cheek.

"Thank you for agreeing to help," I said.

"Don't mention it," Adele said. "We can't afford to lose another chief so soon after Chief O'Neill."

My stomach churned. I hadn't even considered the prospect of actually losing Sawyer to the spell.

Adele peeled back to observe the fox in my arms. "Well,

now. Good to see you, Chief Fox." She scratched the animal's head. "If you don't mind me saying, you make a sweet fox."

"Makes a sweet man, too," Rosalie said. "Too bad my daughter couldn't hold his interest."

Corinne shot her mother a warning glance. "It wasn't like that and you know it."

Rosalie ignored her. Instead, she snapped her fingers at me. "Bring him to the circle."

I walked to the white chalk circle and held the fox up over my head, singing *Circle of Life* from *The Lion King* until Adele silenced me with a look.

"He's cuter than Simba," Rosalie said. She set different-colored candles around the perimeter of the circle. "You'll have to leave him alone in the circle for the spell. Do you think he'll stay or do we need to conjure a ward to keep him inside?"

I placed the fox in the middle of the circle and crouched down to address him. "Chief, it's important that you stay put in the circle during the spell. These lovely ladies are going to try to reverse whatever's been done to you."

"If it's a witch's spell, we should be able to undo it," Corinne said.

"Not necessarily," Adele countered. "It depends on the type of magic and the specific spell that was used."

"Come on, coven," Rosalie said. "Are we LeRoux witches or not? We've got this." She shook her hands to loosen the muscles.

"Let me know if there's anything I can do to help," I said.

"Stand clear, girl," Rosalie said. "Be a real shame if you accidentally got zapped by our spell." She didn't look remotely bothered by the prospect.

"Wouldn't I just remain intact?" I asked. "If you're trying to turn a fox into a human, I don't think I'm in any danger."

Rosalie clapped a hand onto her hip. "So it would be

72

perfectly okay with you if you turned into Chief Fox and the fox stayed a fox?"

"I see your point." I took a long step backward toward the canal.

"Join hands, witches," Adele said.

The witches began to chant, channeling the energy around them. As the wind blew harder, the water wheel began to turn faster and the sound of rushing water filled the air.

"We present to you Sawyer Fox," they said. "This flame draws health and strength back to his body."

I watched as the orange candles lit up.

"This flame draws peace and tranquility to keep his troubled mind at ease."

Flames lit the wicks of the blue candles.

"This flame returns Sawyer Fox to himself, steady and true."

I watched the red candles expectantly, but no light came to them. Disappointment flooded me as I realized the ritual was over and it had failed. The same fox sat in the circle. He observed me with sad eyes and I blinked away tears. The witches broke the circle.

"Why didn't it work?" Corinne asked.

Adele clasped her hands in front of her and studied the fox. "As I said, it could be the type of magic or it could be that it isn't magic at all."

"What do you mean?" Rosalie asked. "He's some kind of shifter?"

"I mean that if another type of supernatural is responsible for this, then our magic will have no effect." Adele shifted her gaze to me. "Perhaps a demon of some sort?"

"My father insists that it's not the work of a vengeance demon," I said. But it could still be the work of another demon. My schedule was going to be busy tomorrow.

Corinne kneeled next to the chief and patted his back reassuringly. "What if we try a different spell? One that doesn't require undoing the underlying one?"

"And what good would that do?" Rosalie asked.

"If we can conjure a spell that allows him to talk," Corinne replied, "then maybe he can tell us what happened."

I wasn't convinced that he would know anything given that I was kissing him on his sofa when it happened, but I couldn't divulge this fact to the LeRoux trio. The potential ramifications were too far-reaching.

"It's worth a try," Adele agreed. She took her place at the circle and wiggled her fingers. The other two joined her and they began a new chant. This spell was less dramatic.

"Magic of the river. Magic of the creek. Grant this fox the power to speak."

"Chief Fox?" Adele said, bending toward him.

The fox opened his mouth, but no sound came out.

Corinne's face fell. "Why is our magic so weak?"

Adele draped an arm along her granddaughter's shoulders. "Our magic is not weak, dearest. It's simply not the right magic for whatever ails him. The wrong shaped key for this hole, if you will."

"I really appreciate that you tried," I said.

"Sorry it didn't work out," Corinne said. "I thought we'd be able to help."

"And what of the chief?" Adele asked.

"Our secret is safe with him," I assured her. "I think it's good to have the head of law enforcement on our side."

"Just because he knows about us doesn't mean he's on our side," Rosalie snapped.

"I agree with Eden," Adele said. "I would have loved for Mick O'Neill to be connected to our community, but he was not the right choice for that bridge." The former chief had been golfing buddies with my father, but the human had no clue that he'd been playing with a vengeance demon.

I faced her. "But you think Chief Fox is?"

She nodded. "I'm willing to entertain the notion."

That made me feel better. It would be helpful to have Adele LeRoux in my corner should my family ever find out about the chief and attempt to ruin his life. I hated that our relationship put him at risk, but the choice was his to make and I respected it.

"I'll see you at the council meeting tomorrow night, Eden," Adele said. "I suppose we'll have a lot to discuss with the others."

She was right. I was going to have to spend tomorrow at the office with Neville, researching demons. I'd been hopeful that I'd have the chief back to normal tonight, and not only for selfish reasons. Worry creeped up my spine.

"You'd better keep searching for an answer," Rosalie said.

I gathered the fox into my arms. "Of course. I'm not going to let him stay like this. It's bad for the town."

Rosalie snorted. "The town. Right. Anyway, the longer this goes on, the greater the chance that he's stuck like this."

I thought of the premature aging spell on my mother. Knowing Grandma, it was the type that would wear off on its own...eventually. She'd just torture my mother with the knowledge that she could make my mother younger again at any time.

"Stuck as in permanently?" I asked.

Rosalie inspected the fox in my arms. "Good thing he supports adoption efforts for stray animals. If we can't find a solution, the chief might need someone to adopt him soon enough."

I couldn't fathom that outcome. I held the fox tightly.

"Rosalie, there's no need to scare the poor girl," Adele said. "We'll work together and find another solution."

"He's not going to be stuck like this. I won't let him," I said. What good was being a fury for the FBM if I couldn't fix a situation like this one? I hurried to the car with the fox in my arms.

"Eden, if you think you can do this alone, you're crazy," Rosalie called after me.

"I sure am," I yelled over my shoulder.

Crazy like a fox.

CHAPTER EIGHT

I PRESSED my hands on the stone walls inside the mound and let the energy wash over me. It felt the same as always, no reason to believe that the dormant portal was now active. My butt began to vibrate. I retrieved the phone from my pocket.

"What's up, Neville?"

"I thought you'd be in the office by now."

"I'm on my way. I decided to stop and check on the portal on my way in. Make sure I didn't miss a leak or something."

"Ah, very well then. Carry on."

"Is Achilles with you?" I asked.

"Yes, we just came back from a walk," the wizard said.

"Okay." I'd have to figure out where to leave the fox if I didn't want to drive all the way home first. The shoebox-sized office was too small to keep both a pug and a fox.

"No need to stop for a latte on your way in," he said. "I've popped in to Holes on the way back from our walk and Paige was kind enough to bestow freebies upon us. She even gave Achilles a puppuccino."

"Yum, I love the taste of freebies."

"He did as well," Neville said. "He had a white mustache and beard until he finally licked it off. I think he was trying to save it for later."

"Sounds adorable. I'll see you soon," I said, and put away the phone. I looked down at the fox. "What do you think? Where should I bring you for safekeeping?"

The fox swished his tail but said nothing.

Who would be crazy enough to want to babysit a fox with no questions asked? A name popped into my head and I smiled. "Let's go, Sawyer. I know a nice room with a view."

The lighthouse was close enough to walk to, so I let the fox trot beside me.

"Cool dog," a little boy said, as we passed by. "Can I pet him?"

"He's not always friendly," I said. "But thanks for asking." Once we were out of earshot, I bent toward the chief. "You're the friendliest guy I know. I just had to say that."

The fox seemed to be smiling as we entered the lighthouse and began the spiraling climb to the top.

"Ted," I called. His name bounced off the cold, hard walls. "It's Eden Fury." I poked my head in the doorway at the top. "Is your cat around because I have a fox with me?"

The older man looked startled. "A fox?"

I angled my head toward the floor, where the fox stood beside me. "This little guy." I cleared my throat. "Sorry, this big guy."

Ted peered at the fox. "Oh, I see. You're in luck. There are no other animals with me at the moment."

"Perfect." I stepped into the round room with its impressive vista of the Chesapeake Bay. "Can I ask a huge favor? I need someone I trust to look after him for me, only for a little while."

The slender man broke into a proud smile. "I'd be honored, Eden. I take it Thora was busy?"

"My house is kind of in chaos right now," I said. "My mom and Grandma are fighting. I don't think it's the best environment for a fox."

Ted slid his hands into his pockets and offered a regretful sigh. "Yes, they do seem to wreak havoc when they argue, don't they?" He leaned down to address the fox. "I'm happy to look after you, sir."

"Thank you so much," I said. "If you wouldn't mind keeping it to yourself, I'd appreciate it. People act weird when they see what they consider to be a wild animal."

"I completely understand," Ted said. "What's his name?"

"Chi…Chicago, but with a hard Ch sound." Inwardly, I cringed. How had I managed to lie my way through my youth? I was woefully out of practice.

"Chicago. Got it." Ted scratched his head. "Does he need anything special to eat?"

"Fruits and raw vegetables are fine, and plenty of water."

"Do I need to walk him outside so he can do his business?"

"No, he can hold it," I said. "I just need to do some work at the office and then I'll collect him."

"Sounds good." Ted shifted his attention to the fox. "Now, Mr. Chicago. I have a few activities to occupy our time. How do you feel about checkers?"

I spun on my heel and raced down the spiral steps. I returned to my car and made the quick drive to the wrong side of the tracks where the office was located. Nestled between a tattoo parlor and a donut shop, the FBM was hardly splurging on prime real estate. I snagged a parking spot out front and checked that the ward was down before entering the office. No need to embarrass myself today by bouncing off the door and into the street. Try explaining that to a human.

"Agent Fury, finally," Neville said.

I pulled a face. "You act like I was lounging around in my pj's, feeding potato chips out of the bag to my boyfriend in my attic paradise."

His brow lifted. "That sounds awfully specific."

"I told you I was checking the portal and I was." Besides, we finished off the bag of potato chips this morning. Chief Fox is a huge fan of salt and vinegar chips, apparently.

"Your beverage is on your desk," he said. "Mind the temperature."

"Ooh, and a bear claw too." A bark sounded from the back of the room and I waved to Achilles. "How was your treat? I bet it was delicious."

Achilles barked in response.

"I guess there was no breakthrough if you're here alone," Neville said.

"Unfortunately not," I said, dropping into my chair and booting up my computer. "The witches couldn't break the spell."

"Then what's on the agenda?" he asked.

I swiveled my chair to face him. "Talk to me about demons," I said. "Which ones can turn humans into animals?"

Neville rubbed his cheek. "Quite a few, actually. It's not an uncommon ability. You also can't rule out wizards, warlocks, and other magical beings."

"I can when I know every one of them within a twenty-mile radius," I said.

"Have you talked to your cousin?" Neville asked. "He's a pretty talented warlock."

"Rafael? What reason could he possibly have to turn the chief into a fox?"

"Maybe he and the chief had an interaction regarding the restaurant." It is universally acknowledged that the best restaurant in Chipping Cheddar is Chophouse, which happens to be owned and operated by Rafael, a fastidious chef.

"No way. Chief Fox would've mentioned it, and Rafael would've complained to everyone in my family about the injustice."

"What about your brother?" Neville asked. "He's a vengeance demon that could risk doing something in town without your father's blessing."

I burst into laughter. "Anton? Why would he want to transform the chief?"

"You were worried about your family finding out," he said. "Maybe you were focused on the wrong members."

I shook my head. "Anton is way too laidback to care, and he doesn't share my mother's attitude. He's more tolerant."

"I guess he'd have to be. He married a druid."

My head jerked toward him. "What's that supposed to mean?"

"Nothing," Neville said quickly. "I only meant that your parents wouldn't be thrilled with a druid for a daughter-in-law."

"You're right about that. To be fair, Verity doesn't love having them as in-laws either. She's more like me." One reason we got along so well. "I think a demon is our best bet. Have you read the latest reports from Otherworld?"

"Yes. There are no escaped demons that match what we're looking for," Neville said.

"Then let's see what we can find in the FBM database." I heard the clickety clack of Neville's new mechanical keyboard as he typed enthusiastically. "You sound like you and your horse are riding into town to hit up the saloon."

Neville kept his gaze on the screen. "I like the sound. I find it soothing."

"And I'm going to need noise-canceling headphones."

"I'm sending you a list of options," he said. "You take the first half and I'll take the second."

"Okey doke." I opened the link on my computer and started with the first entry. "An animal demon? It can't be that simple. That's too on-the-nose." I clicked on the entry and read the summary. "This demon leaves a distinct smell of wet dog fur in its wake." I contemplated the description. "I didn't smell any wet dogs when the chief turned into a fox."

"Here's one," Neville said. "A Cailleach demon." He frowned. "No, wait. That demon can disguise himself as a fox, not other people."

"Well, I doubt the chief has been a secret Cailleach demon all this time," I said.

"Can we discuss your catchphrase while we research? We're both good at multitasking."

"No one's good at multitasking. It's a lie we tell ourselves to feel more productive." I leaned my head back and looked at him. "Neville, seriously. It's not like I'm a superhero. A catchphrase isn't necessary."

"Of course not. It is, however, fun."

"Spider-Man doesn't have a catchphrase and he's awesome, so I don't think I need one."

Neville folded his arms, indignant. "He certainly does. He says he's the friendly neighborhood Spider-Man."

I craned my neck to look at him. "I don't think that qualifies as a catchphrase."

Neville's eyes glimmered with hope. "How about 'let's get fast and fury-ous?'"

I fixed Neville with a hairy eyeball. "Cut it out. I don't need a catchphrase."

The wizard slumped in his chair. "And here I thought you were adventurous."

"I'll be more open to discussing this once Chief Fox is back to normal. This whole thing is stressing me out. Rosalie has me worried that he's going to be trapped like this forever."

"I can see why that might distress you."

Neville began typing again and I tried to block out the sound. I continued to check the links on my half of the list. Many were easy to dismiss because the telltale signs were missing.

"An Inari demon sounds promising," I said. "They use foxes as messengers. Maybe a demon changed the chief into a fox to serve as a messenger."

"Then what's the message?" Neville asked.

I chewed my lip, wracking my brain for a sensible response. "I have no idea. Not very effective as a communication tool, is it?"

"Are we certain the chief isn't a secret kitsune?" Neville asked. "Maybe he didn't know and something happened to trigger the shift?"

"Like what—true love's kiss?" I joked, snorting with laughter. The laughter stopped abruptly and I touched my fingers to my lips. Great Goddess! What if it *was* something like that?

Neville peered at me, curious. "What is it, Agent Fury?"

"Is that possible?" I asked. "Could the chief be a shifter without realizing it?" And, if so, why couldn't he shift back? Did he need to be taught?

"I suppose it's possible," Neville said. "There are plenty of stories about women who don't realize they're witches until they're older or something dramatic happens to trigger their magic."

"Wizards too," I said. "Harry Potter didn't know he was a wizard until he was eleven."

Neville scoffed. "Harry Potter? Be serious. I'm talking about *real* witches and wizards, Agent Fury."

Achilles waddled between our desks and plopped onto

the floor in a bid for attention. I felt a tug of sympathy. The poor pug had to be missing his human companion. I knew I sure was. I wheeled over to him and leaned down to rub his belly.

"You should think about getting a dog, Neville."

"I prefer my canine interactions to be brief but meaningful," the wizard replied.

I glanced at him. "What does that even mean? You seem to enjoy having Achilles around. And you already discovered he's a magnet for women."

Neville smiled. "Indeed I did. All this time I thought it was simply fodder for sitcoms."

"If you don't want the daily responsibility, you could apply to foster dogs while they wait for permanent homes."

Neville gazed thoughtfully at the pug. "That's actually an excellent idea,"

I bristled. "Try not to sound so surprised." I rolled back to my desk and continued reading about the relevant demons.

"What about an ancestral spirit?" Neville asked. "This area was once inhabited by Native American tribes. Perhaps it's some sort of message."

"If that's the case, then they waited an awfully long time to express their displeasure," I said. "The original Puritans are long gone." Which reminded me that I needed to talk to Alice about the secret club for Clara's article.

"You're right," Neville said. "It doesn't fit the description anyway."

I leaned my elbow on the desk, weary from reading. "I hate to say it, but I think the secret shifter is our best theory right now," I said.

"Would it be so terrible?" Neville asked. "It would mean the acceptance of your family and automatic inclusion in the supernatural world. It solves your two main issues right there."

That was true. Although my family didn't love shifters, the awesomeness of Julie and Meg robbed them of any meaningful objection. It would still be difficult to have the head of law enforcement as my boyfriend while quietly battling my family's evil tendencies, but definitely easier than the current situation.

"I guess it would have its perks," I admitted. My phone lit up and I spied a text from my mother. Uh oh. I picked up the phone to read the missive.

I need you to stop at the store on your way home since your grandmother refuses to undo the hex. We're having company for dinner and I need a bag of potatoes and three pounds of stewing beef.

"She never asks," I mumbled.

"Never asks what?"

"My mother. She tells me instead of asks me," I said. I typed back—*No problem. Are you sure you want to entertain in your condition?*

It's only family. I'd rather die than let your grandmother get the better of me.

Fair enough.

Each one was as stubborn as the other. "I have to go soon. I need to go to the store first, then grab the fox, then drive home. Are you okay to take Achilles again?"

Neville sorted through paperwork from the printer. "Absolutely."

I gave him a grateful smile. "Thanks, you're the best."

CHAPTER NINE

I ARRIVED home with two bags of groceries. I'd snuck the fox into the barn for now, until it was safe to retrieve him. John was gone for the day so there was no chance of scaring him. Aunt Thora stood at the island in the kitchen, chopping celery and carrots.

"Who's coming for dinner?" I asked.

"Moyer and Tomas, and your brother with his family," Aunt Thora replied. "It was already on the calendar so your mother decided not to cancel, despite her current condition."

"Did she forget I have my supernatural council meeting tonight?"

Aunt Thora offered a sympathetic look. "You'll have to ask her."

"I can stay for a bit," I said. "Hopefully I'll get to eat, but no coffee and conversation afterward."

"You'll be missed." Aunt Thora started to remove the packages from the bags. "Perfect. I need to get the stew going or it won't be ready in time. It might need a magical boost."

"I thought my mother was cooking."

Aunt Thora said nothing as she opened the package of meat and emptied it into the large pot.

"You're not obliged to do everything for them, you know," I said. "You're not a servant here."

Aunt Thora washed her hands. "And I suppose you've confronted them about Tanner." She dried her hands on the dishcloth.

"I've been considering it," I said. "The timing isn't right. Besides, I don't want to get you in trouble."

"Then don't tell them I was responsible for squealing. I don't want to end up buried under a lemon tree, not until I'm truly dead anyway."

"Is that the real reason you created the murder jar?" I asked. "A precaution?"

She shrugged. "I thought it was a good idea either way."

"You thought what was a good idea?" My mother sauntered into the kitchen and I had to do a double-take. She wore her white hair in a sleek, straight style and a black dress that showed off the slightly curvier figure that came with age.

"Someone's embraced her new appearance," I remarked.

My mother plucked a grape from the fruit bowl and chewed. "If you think for one second that I'll let Grandma win, you'd best think again. I'm going to be the sexiest, most confident old lady this town has ever seen. She'll be so irritated that she'll turn me back."

I had to hand it to Beatrice Fury. She was determined to be true to herself no matter what obstacles she faced. Even her magically-induced wrinkles seemed smoother. I'd envy her if she didn't annoy me so much.

"What time will everyone be here?" I asked.

"Sooner than dinner will be ready," my mother said. "What was the delay, Aunt Thora?"

"She doesn't work for you," I said.

My mother gave me a demure smile. "Honey, everybody works for me in their own way."

The doorbell rang, saving my mother from having her magic siphoned. I couldn't hex her without a magical boost, but I could drain her dry for the rest of the evening. Let's see how her wrinkles handled that.

Anton bustled into the kitchen, accompanied by Verity and the children. Uncle Moyer followed closely behind with his husband, Tomas, an angel-human hybrid.

"Look at the trouble we ran into outside," Uncle Moyer said. "For once, everyone's on time." He kissed his mother on the cheek and Aunt Thora beamed at the sight of him.

"It was close," Tomas admitted. "I left a trail of angel dust on the carpet and Moyer nearly had a coronary. He insisted on hauling out the vacuum and sucking it up before we could leave."

"The cleaners had just been to the house this morning," the demonic lawyer replied. "Can we at least keep it clean for a whole twenty-four hours? Is that too much to ask?"

Aunt Thora smiled. "That brings back memories. I still remember Moyer presenting his and Charisma's dolls with a list of rules they had to abide by if they expected to live in the playroom."

Tomas gave his husband an affectionate squeeze. "Heaven have mercy. You had to be the most adorable demon child that ever roamed the earth."

"How is Charisma?" I asked. Aunt Thora's daughter lived in Florida with her husband, Marty. We didn't see them often.

"Her skin is about the same color as my leather loafers," Uncle Moyer said. "And the same texture too."

"Now, Moyer," Aunt Thora admonished him. "You be nice. Your sister's not here to defend herself."

"Speaking of defending ourselves…" Tomas twirled around to confront my mother. "Do you have anything to say, gorgeous, or are we supposed to pretend we don't notice you?"

My mother gave him a sly look. "Honey, it's impossible not to notice me."

"You got that right." Olivia marched straight up to my mother with her hands cemented on her small hips. "Why do you look so old?"

Ryan laughed and pointed. I couldn't decide whether he was a toddler or a Mean Girl in training.

"You can thank Great-Grandma," my mother replied. "She thought it would be a good joke to make me old before my time."

"You wear it well," Verity said.

My mother smoothed the ruched fabric along her hips. "Don't I though?"

Anton crunched on a piece of celery. "You're not considering leaving the house like that, are you?"

"Why? Are you embarrassed by my appearance?" my mother asked.

"No, but aren't you?" Anton asked.

I sucked in a breath. Uh oh. Wrong answer. I pretended to slice my neck and Anton quickly realized his mistake.

"What I mean to say is, how will you explain this to people you know?"

My mother fluffed her hair. "I've decided to go incognito. Call myself Brenda. Try out a new personality while I'm at it."

"I think we could all benefit from that," Grandma said, as she shuffled into the room.

My mother rounded on her, pointing an angry finger. "No comments from you this evening."

"Ha! I'd like to see you make that happen." Grandma

brushed past her and reached for a slice of cheese on the island.

My mother's coral-colored lips curved into a malicious smile. "Challenge accepted." She made a zipping motion with her finger.

Please no.

Grandma's eyes widened as she tried to shove the cheese into her mouth and realized she couldn't.

"Beatrice, I'm not sure this is a good idea," Uncle Moyer said.

"Hush, Moyer," my mother said. "It's a spell I should've done from the start. When she undoes my spell, I'll undo hers."

"I thought you were happy with your new look," Anton said.

"Oh, be quiet, Anton," my mother huffed. "How could any woman be happy looking like Santa Claus's younger sister? I want my body back."

Hmm. For once, a standoff between the two of them could work in my favor. With my mother prematurely old and Grandma unable to speak, they'd likely be too distracted by their own obstacles to pay attention to me.

As Anton stepped forward to intervene, I put a hand on his shoulder to still him. He shot me a quizzical look, but I only shook my head.

"Why is Great-Grandma's face so red?" Olivia asked. "She looks like a lava globe."

That was an apt description. At least if she erupted, the fallout would be directed at one particular witch. In the meantime, the house was going to be very uncomfortable until this issue was resolved. Unfortunately, they were the two most stubborn women I'd ever known.

"You're welcome to stay with us until this blows over, Mom," Tomas said to Aunt Thora.

She patted his cheek. "You're an angel."

Tomas smiled. "Well, only half."

Grandma rose to her feet and everyone tensed, waiting to see what would happen next. Olivia seemed to sense the impending catastrophe because she kept glancing from Grandma to my mother. Ryan pushed his chunky body into an upright position and toddled over to Grandma. I held my breath, hoping that he wouldn't do something to exacerbate the situation. My boyfriend was already a fox. I didn't need my nephew to become a toad. If this kept up, I'd have an entire menagerie at my disposal.

The toddler dug around in his pocket and produced a half-eaten cookie. He held it up to Grandma in his sticky, chubby hand. A peace offering.

"Great-Grandma can't eat that right now, sweetheart," Verity said, "but I'm sure she wouldn't mind saving it for later."

The longer Grandma kept her gaze fixed on Ryan, the calmer she seemed. Finally, she reached out and accepted the cookie. Ryan gurgled his delight and clapped his hands. Grandma gave my mother a parting glance as she left the room, still clutching the broken cookie.

The tension in the room dissolved.

Tomas leaned against Uncle Moyer. "Fabulous. He's a Witch Whisperer."

Now that Grandma had retreated to her room, my mother perked up. She clearly felt that she'd won the battle, but I was more worried about the war.

"Who's hungry?" my mother asked. "Those of us with working mouths should eat." She practically skipped over to the table and planted herself in the head chair.

Olivia climbed into the seat adjacent to hers. "That wasn't very nice."

My mother seemed taken aback. "Well, Olivia. I'm a witch. Not everything I do will be nice."

"Why can't you be a white witch?" Olivia asked. "They're nice. And they sparkle."

My mother glared at Verity. "What kind of nonsense are you teaching this child?"

Verity shot a guilty look at Anton. "Olivia's in school, don't forget. She's exposed to a lot of different ideas."

My mother leaned forward so that her face was close to Olivia's. "This family is not in the business of being nice. Do you understand?"

Olivia appeared unfazed by my mother's intimidation tactic. "Why not?"

"Why not?" my mother sputtered. She reeled back, surprised by the question.

"Why can't we be nice?" Olivia pressed. "Does it hurt us?"

My chest ached with hope. I knew my parents were keen to have Olivia and Ryan embrace the dark side of supernatural life, but they were showing signs of rebellion at young ages. It was encouraging to witness.

"Because we are powerful supernaturals," my mother said. "We use black magic because it's the most potent."

"What does potent mean?" Olivia asked.

"Powerful," Verity said.

Olivia folded her arms in a huff. "Then I don't want to be powerful. I want to be the opposite. Unpotent."

"Impotent," Anton corrected her and immediately turned a shade of red.

"Oh, you don't want that," Uncle Moyer interjected.

"Nobody wants that," Tomas chimed in.

My mother narrowed her eyes at Verity. "This has your sappy druid fingerprints all over it."

Anton swooped into the chair across the table. "Mother, we don't need to assign blame…"

My mother's head swiveled toward him. "How are these kids going to survive in the world if they're hellbent on being nice?" She hissed at the word 'nice,' as though the mere mention of it burned her tongue.

"We're not having this discussion right now," Anton said. "We came over for a pleasant family dinner. If you're going to have a meltdown over the way we're choosing to raise our kids, we'll go home and enjoy our dinner in peace and quiet."

My mother slammed a hand on the table. "A-ha! So you are choosing to raise them this way. I knew it."

Anton rolled his eyes. "Don't twist my words."

"By the devil, you're a vengeance demon," she seethed. "What's the matter with you? We didn't raise you to care about others' feelings. I told your father it was a mistake to let you attend public school. We should have sent you to boarding school in Otherworld."

I shuddered at the thought. What kind of fury would I have become if I'd grown up in Otherworld? Probably the kind that got hunted by FBM agents.

"I'm in the midst of an interesting legal battle," Uncle Moyer said, as he helped his mother distribute the appetizers. Verity shot him a grateful look.

"Aren't you always in a legal battle?" Anton asked. "You're a lawyer."

"Yes, but this time I'm suing a former client," he said. "She came to me—pitiful thing—desperate for me to acquire her soul in exchange for a favor."

"Sounds like a typical transaction," my mother said. "What makes it interesting?"

"Ariel is a natural redhead," he practically spat. "I want to sue for breach of contract and false representation."

"Redheads have no soul," Olivia exclaimed.

"Exactly," Uncle Moyer said. "The trickster colored her

hair black before the meeting. I had no idea I was dealing with a ginger."

"That was either incredibly brave or incredibly stupid," my mother said. "Did she think you wouldn't find out?"

"I think she believed she'd be long gone by then," Uncle Moyer said. "But the truth has a way of finding the cracks and filtering through."

"Those are called roots," Tomas quipped.

"I want to see Aunt Eden's new house," Olivia said. She gripped a knife and fork in each hand and banged them on the table.

My heart jumped. "That's not a good idea right now, Olivia. There are lots of tools lying around because John's nearly finished."

"I can shine a spotlight," Anton said. "It'll be fine."

I hesitated, trying to come up with a reasonable excuse. "I'd rather wait until it's completely done so I can show it off properly. It would be nice to get furniture."

"Oh, I know the perfect place to furniture shop," Moyer said. "There's a wonderful antique shop in town called Treasure Trove."

"That sounds promising," I said. "Where is it?"

"Behind that Indian takeout place," he said. "You can douse yourself in the scent of curry as you go in and it will cling to you for the rest of the day."

"I happen to like the smell of curry," Tomas said. "I don't mind that he wears it like a fragrance."

"Foster is a friendly," Uncle Moyer said.

"He's one of us?" I asked.

"No, but he has the Sight," Uncle Moyer said. "I think it's part of the reason he's so good at finding antiques. He sees beauty that other humans overlook."

"That's a nice way of putting it," I said.

Dinner was too far behind schedule for me to wait to eat.

I shoved another carrot stick in my mouth and chewed hungrily. Quickly, I washed it down with a glass of home-made lemonade.

"Well, it's been fun, but I'm expected at a council meeting"— I checked the clock on my phone— "in about ten minutes."

"Lucky you," Anton grumbled.

I kissed Olivia and Ryan on their heads and grabbed my purse from the kitchen counter. "Don't wait up."

And whatever you do, don't go in the barn.

CHAPTER TEN

I BREEZED into Chophouse and immediately spotted Julie and Meg, along with Ava, Meg's new friend, at a table close to the kitchen. I maneuvered my way through the clusters of other tables to greet them.

"Ooh, is that carrot cake?" I asked. I'd missed out on dessert at the family dinner, so maybe I'd order a slice of heaven here. Rafael took great pride in his culinary creations.

"With cream cheese frosting," Meg said.

I tried not to salivate. "Is there any other kind?"

Ava sliced the entire top of frosting off her cake and covered her fork with it. "It's like eating a sugar cloud. I didn't know this taste existed in the world."

"It's magical," Julie said, with a wink at me. "There's a meeting tonight, huh?"

"Unfortunately," I said. "Believe me, I'd much rather be watching reruns of *Friends*." At least I had a mission to accomplish during this particular meeting, which made attendance worthwhile. If I managed a breakthrough with the chief, it would be worth it.

"What kind of meeting are you going to?" Ava asked. She licked the last of the frosting off her fork.

"Oh, a book club," I said quickly. "We meet in the back room of the restaurant."

"Cool," Ava said. "I love to read. Which book are you discussing tonight?"

"Some rich white guy's autobiography," I said. "Really dull. I'll need a cup of coffee to make it through the meeting."

"Maybe next time you'll get to choose the book," Ava said. "My mom used to be in a book group in our old town and they let another member choose each month." Ava pulled out her phone. "That reminds me. I promised I'd call my mom and tell her what time to expect me home."

Julie smacked Meg's arm. "See? She uses technology to communicate with her mother so that there's no fear that she's been kidnapped or died in a ditch."

Meg's face turned stony. "Mom, please don't embarrass me in front of my friend."

"And you're going to call? Not even text?" Julie asked, impressed.

"She likes to hear my voice," Ava said. "She says you can't tell tone from a text."

"Your mother sounds very wise," Julie said. "I hope I get to meet her soon."

"She'd like that. She hasn't really met any new friends since we moved here. She says I'm lucky because I get to go to school and have forced interaction, but she has to make small talk in the cereal aisle."

"She's not wrong," Julie said. "It can be hard for mothers of older friends to make friends. We're not congregating at the park with our strollers and coffee anymore."

"Excuse me just a sec." Ava tapped her screen and turned away from the table to talk to her mother.

Julie crooked a finger, beckoning me closer. "I heard a rumor about the chief," she said, lowering her voice.

My palms broke into a sweat and I wiped them on my pant legs. Had we not been careful enough? Had someone seen us together before his transformation? "Heard what?"

Julie inclined her head toward the back room. "I assume it's what you'll be discussing in the meeting."

Did she think I needed the council's permission to date him? "You know I can't divulge our topics of discussion."

She lowered her voice. "Fine, but if people are turning into foxes, then we need to be told, especially the shifter community. What if we accidentally hurt someone that we think is prey?"

Phew. "How did you hear about it? No one's supposed to know."

"I told her." Rafael appeared beside me.

I cut a glance at my cousin. "How did you find out?"

"I run a busy restaurant, Eden. It's as gossipy as a hair salon. You know that."

I gripped the back of my chair and looked at him with pleading eyes. "Please don't tell anyone in my family. Not a word."

"Not to worry," he said. "I won't say a thing. I know how serious it can be if word gets around. To be honest, I haven't seen anyone in over a week. Thora was in here with Ted O'Neill and that's the last time I saw anyone." A smile touched his lips. "You have to admire a woman that brings her own lemons to the restaurant."

I squinted at him. "Do you?" Aunt Thora's obsession with lemons bordered on insanity. It was bad enough when customers brought their own teabags and sugar packets.

"They were fresher than anything I had in stock," Rafael said. "And you know I take great pride in my masterpieces."

"Oh, I know." Rafael sliced and diced his ingredients like

he was preparing the contents of a cauldron for a ravenous coven. His precision with a blade was unparalleled. If you needed surgery on a newt's eye, he was your warlock.

Ava turned back to the table. "Mom seems happy that I'm being social."

"It must be hard," Julie said. "I can't imagine trying to fit in somewhere new at this point in your education. You must be thinking 'what's the point' because you'll be heading to college soon anyway."

Ava stuffed her phone back into her small, sparkly purse. "I guess, but it's more pleasant to pass the time with friends. Besides, I'm not sure I want to go to college."

Julie nearly choked on her mouthful of cake. "I'm sorry. Is that an option?"

Meg gave her mother a hard look. "Mom, college isn't for everyone. Don't be so judgmental."

"I'm not being judgmental." Julie gulped down her water to clear her throat. "I just think a degree is important in this world no matter what your future plans are."

"See? Judgmental." Meg turned to her friend. "Don't listen to her, Ava. College is overpriced and overrated."

"I'm going to pretend I didn't hear that," Julie said.

My gaze drifted to the back room. "Well, it was nice seeing you, but I'd better get in there since I'm already late."

"Enjoy your meeting," Ava said.

I hurried to the back of the restaurant and slipped into the private room. Four heads snapped toward me when I entered the room—Adele, Aggie Grace, Husbourne Crawley, and Hugh Phelps.

"How's the chief?" Husbourne drawled in his Foghorn Leghorn accent. The white wizard watched me expectantly.

"I told them," Adele said. "I thought it best to put the urgent matter at the top of the agenda."

"The chief's safe," I said. "I've got Princess Buttercup

keeping an eye on him." She wouldn't hesitate to use her acidic drool as a weapon if it came down to it. She may look like a Great Dane to humans, but the hellhound was no gentle giant if one of her loved ones was under threat. Right now, Chief Fox fell into that category.

"Does your family know?" Husbourne asked and adjusted the lapel of his seersucker suit. Husbourne lived on Munster Close and knew my family well—probably better than he wanted to.

"Definitely not," I said. "And I'd very much like to keep it that way."

"I take it you've checked the portal," Aggie said. She also lived on our cul-de-sac with her two sisters and I'd spent an inordinate amount of my childhood in their backyard oasis.

"The portal is secure," I said. "Neville and I have been researching potential demons with this sort of ability but nothing matches, and there've been no reports of escaped demons from Otherworld that fit the description." I started to say more, but Hugh's expression stopped me.

"Hmm," he said, and stroked the stubble on his rugged jawline.

"What?" I asked.

"What do we know about Sawyer Fox?" he asked. "He's new to Chipping Cheddar. Maybe he's made enemies that have followed him to our bucolic town."

"The thought occurred to me," I said. "We checked his records in Iowa and it's outstanding. Plus, he's human. He hasn't gotten tangled up in any supernatural messes." Until he met me, of course.

"None that he knows of," Husbourne said. "Hugh is right. Maybe the chief got mixed up with supernaturals without realizing it."

I gave an adamant shake of my head. "We're barking up

the wrong tree." I cut a quick glance at the werewolf. "No offense."

"Then you've settled on a demon?" Aggie pressed.

"Not necessarily," I said.

Adele regarded me. "What is it, Eden? Another theory?"

"I'm probably grasping at straws at this point, but it's worth pursuing." I faced Hugh. "I have a favor to ask."

He leaned forward, eyeing me appreciatively. "I'm a married wolf, Eden, but I'm sure I could make an exception for the sake of a lesson or two."

"Pipe down, my boy, before we neuter you right on the table," Husbourne said, sounding disgusted.

"Neville and I are wondering if the chief is a secret shifter," I said.

"Wouldn't we have figured that out by now?" Aggie asked.

"What if he didn't know?" I said. "What if he was human until something triggered the change?"

"Like a werefox bite?" Adele said.

"What else could trigger a change like that?" Aggie asked.

Husbourne took a sip of nectar, the homemade recipe that kicked off all supernatural council meetings. "A broken spell."

"A broken spell?" Hugh queried. "What do you mean?"

"Perhaps someone used magic to hide his shifter side," Husbourne said. "Such a thing isn't unheard of."

"And then something happened that broke the spell," Adele said. "Maybe that explains why we couldn't change him back."

I looked at Hugh. "I'd like you to try to teach the chief how to shift. If he really is some kind of secret kitsune or werefox trapped in animal form, then maybe he doesn't know how to get himself back to human form."

Hugh popped an olive into his mouth. "I suppose I could

do that, although the transformation is fairly intuitive. If he's a shifter, he should be able to change naturally."

"Not if he's never done it before," I countered. "He didn't even know the supernatural world existed…until now. He's not going to know how to shift."

"Unless he lied," Hugh said. "Men do that, you know."

"Everybody lies," Aggie said. "I've lived long enough to say that with certainty."

"Look, we have to try everything, right?" I said. "We can't have Chief Fox stuck as an animal forever."

"Can't we?" Hugh shrugged. "I'm not sure it's such an issue."

Aggie swatted his arm. "Of course it's an issue, you halfwit. Eden's right. We can't leave the head of law enforcement in a form he isn't meant to stay in, and, if he's one of us, all the more reason to assist him."

"He's not one of us," the werewolf insisted. "I would've smelled it on him. You would have sensed it, Eden."

"If he didn't know it about himself, I doubt anyone would've sensed it," I argued.

He balanced an olive on his nose and then launched it into the air before snatching it with his powerful jaws. "Tell me where and when." He'd obviously mistaken the olive for one without a pit because I heard a cracking sound and he winced in pain. "My tooth."

I bit back a smile. "The barn behind my house tomorrow at nine."

He winced. "Nine sounds very early."

"The carpenter comes at ten, so we need to clear out before he arrives." John had a tendency to sleep late on his boat, not that I blamed him. He was living the dream.

"And what do we do once we resolve the issue?" Husbourne asked. He plucked a toothpick from one of the olives and gnawed on the end.

I swiveled toward him. "What do you mean?"

"I mean, once the chief is back to normal—whatever that may be—do we enlighten him about us?"

The council members exchanged wary glances.

"What if he isn't a secret shifter?" Aggie asked.

"Then we should have a vampire wipe his memory of these events," Hugh said. "Let those fangers be good for something in this town."

I wiggled uncomfortably. Now was the ideal time to broach the subject, no matter how anxious it made me. "What if we didn't wipe his memory?"

"Why wouldn't we?" Aggie asked. "Human law enforcement has always been ignorant of our kind."

"But I think he would be an asset," I said. "Why keep him in the dark?"

"That's obvious," Husbourne said. "Because he's human. It's too much for them. They can't handle someone tearing away the veil. Be like snatching a child's security blanket."

Except Sawyer had already proven that he could handle it. "I propose that we put it to a vote. Husbourne, you're our eyes and ears on the town council. Why not let Chief Fox be our eyes and ears in law enforcement?"

"Because you're our eyes and ears in law enforcement," Hugh said. "That's the whole point of the FBM outpost."

"No, the whole point of the outpost is to monitor the portal," I said. "Looking out for supernatural interferences is secondary."

Adele stroked the pearls around her neck. "He's been involved in a few supernatural incidents already without his knowledge and he handled himself remarkably well."

"What about his deputy?" Hugh asked. "We're going to expect him to keep it secret from that gonad, aren't we? He's too stupid to share information as important as this."

"Deputy Guthrie is a hard pass," Husbourne drawled, making a sideways chopping motion with his hand.

"I think we can trust the chief," I said, "especially after we rescue him from whatever situation he's gotten himself into. He'll feel indebted to us." I figured it couldn't hurt to throw an extra reason in there.

Aggie rubbed her hands together in a nervous gesture. "Oh, my. This would be unprecedented. We've never had a member of law enforcement in the know." She drew a breath. "But I agree with Eden, I think Chief Fox would be an asset to the council, as well as to the supernatural community at large. Think about it. He'll be able to assess a situation and recognize whether he can handle it or whether he needs to call for supernatural reinforcements. Chief O'Neill didn't have that luxury."

"If he had, maybe he'd still be alive today," Adele said. "I think it's in everyone's best interest, including the chief's."

"All in favor?" Aggie asked.

I watched as each hand went up. Hugh hesitated for a fleeting moment, but I was pretty sure it was only to be difficult.

"Perfect," I said.

My phone vibrated in my purse and I rooted around the black hole of small belongings until I found it. "Hello?"

"Eden, it's Sean." He cleared his throat. "It's Deputy Guthrie."

Speak of the gonad. "Is everything okay?"

"Not really," he said.

I closed my eyes and prayed to every deity in existence that Sawyer was all right. "What happened?"

"It's about that snake."

I perked up. "What about it?"

"Meet me at that lady's house. The one who reported the sighting."

"Eloise Worthington?" I asked.

"That's the one. Do you remember the address?"

"I do." I hesitated to ask my next question. "Did you find the snake?"

"No, but it looks like the snake found her," Sean said. "Eloise is dead."

CHAPTER ELEVEN

I GAPED at the scene in the foyer of Eloise Worthington's house. A baseball bat lay next to Eloise's body and shards of broken glass covered the floor. It looked like she'd tried to throw everything within reach at her attacker. I even noticed pieces of kibble mixed in with the shards. Even amidst the chaos, I couldn't help but notice Eloise's appearance.

"Why is she wearing a hot dog costume?" I asked.

"She was known for it," Sean said. "I didn't actually realize it was the same woman until I got here."

I studied the hot dog on the floor. A yellow line of mustard ran up her middle. "She was known for dressing like a hot dog?"

"She'd wear it in front of businesses to protest stuff like poor customer service." Sean shook his head. "I got called to the bank once to cite her for harassment."

"Well, I have to agree with her there. The bank's customer service is terrible."

Sean looked at me. "She was protesting the fact that they'd run out of grape lollipops and could only offer orange."

I stuffed my hands into my pockets and observed the dead woman. "Orange *is* the devil's work."

"You two would've been a nightmare together."

I ignored him. "Are you sure it was the snake that killed her?"

He pointed to her arm. "Puncture wounds equals snake bite. Poisonous too."

"You mean venomous."

"Same thing," he said dismissively.

"No, it isn't."

"Whatever, Professor Fury," he scoffed. "I have a degree too, you know."

"In massive douchebaggery?"

He glowered at me.

"Oh, that was your minor. Got it." I shifted my focus back to Eloise. "How did you even know to come here?"

"She called to say she'd seen the snake and asked me to come," he said. "I guess I wasn't fast enough." He shifted a few shards of glass with the front of his shoe.

"What ever happened to Animal Control?" I asked.

He shrugged. "They haven't had any luck finding it. Seems smart for a snake."

I crouched down for a closer look at the puncture wound. Sean didn't realize that more than a snake could cause a mark like that. There was no evidence of blood and Eloise seemed to have retained hers, so a vampire was unlikely.

I returned to a standing position. "Where's the cat? Mischief?"

Sean shrugged. "Who cares? We have a dead woman in front of us."

I gasped. "Who cares? There's a killer snake on the loose and that cat is the right size for a snack."

He observed me. "Why is the cat's fate more pressing than the woman's?"

"For starters, the cat is still alive." I hoped. If Mischief was anything like Grandma's cat Candy, then she could handle herself, so maybe the cat would be okay. Then again, Eloise had a baseball bat and still ended up dead on the foyer floor. It must've been a sneaky snake attack. "Is there any other evidence? How did the snake get in?" It wasn't as though Eloise would've invited the creature inside for tea and biscuits.

"I haven't noticed an entry point." Sean paled, making his freckles even more prominent. "Do you think it's some kind of velociraptor snake that's smart enough to open doors?"

I fought the desire to smack my forehead—and his. "No, Sean. I don't think we need to call in Jeff Goldblum anytime soon." Not that I would object to actual Jeff Goldblum. He was an icon.

"We'll have to ask the neighborhood to be on alert," Sean said.

I gazed at Eloise's lifeless body. "They're going to be devastated to lose one of their own."

"I don't know," Sean said. "The neighbors didn't have very nice things to say about Eloise the last time we were here."

My jaw unhinged. "So her death is no big deal?"

"I didn't mean it that way," Sean said. "I just don't think there will be any candlelight vigils." He scribbled a few notes on a pad of paper. "Whatever went down here was vicious. That snake was out for blood."

"I don't think that's how snakes work," I said.

"Could've fooled me. Eloise fought hard." He rubbed his hand along his brow. "We need to find this snake before it hurts someone else."

"Or their cat," I added.

He looked at me askance. "You really need to chill out about the animals."

"I'd like to hear you say that in front of Chief Fox." The

chief had single-handedly boosted adoption numbers among rescue dogs in town when he started taking them out on patrol with him. Even Sean had been forced to partake, although it seemed unfair for the dog to be paired with the deputy.

"I wish I could say anything in front of the chief right now," Sean said. "I don't like being out of contact. Is he any closer to getting better? I should call him again and let him know…" He started to tap on his phone and I placed my hand over his.

"The doctor says he needs to rest more than anything. A phone call like this will upset him and delay his progress."

"He has to know about the death of a resident."

"It's an accidental death, Sean, not murder." I paused. "Why not text him? That way, he can choose to read it when he's feeling better." And I knew for a fact that the fox couldn't access any text messages, so there was no chance of Sawyer the fox freaking out. I'd break the news gently.

"Good idea."

The beginning cords of *Back in Black* emanated from the back pocket of my jeans and I groaned.

"Aren't you going to answer that?" Sean asked.

"Answer what?"

"Your butt."

I ignored the music. "Nope."

"That's a good song," Sean said. "I'm surprised you're into it."

"I'm not into it," I said. "It's meant to signify the blackness of my mother's soul."

He arched an eyebrow. "I thought you might have changed now that you're a hotshot FBI agent, but you're still weird."

The song stopped and started three times before I finally

answered the call. "What's the emergency?" I demanded. "I'm in the middle of an emergency."

"So am I." My mother's voice sounded frantic. "The lightbulb's gone out on the paddle fan and I need your man hands to deal with the screwing."

"I would've thought the screwing part was right up your alley," I said.

"Don't you sass me while I'm in my final witch form," she threatened.

"You're not back to your old…I mean, young self yet?" I smiled at Sean, so that he thought I was simply teasing my mother.

"Your grandmother is about to buy a one-way ticket to the burial ground," my mother ground out.

"Please don't," I said.

"I'd call Anton, but it happened after he left and you know that Verity won't let him come back to help his poor mother." She blew an annoyed breath into the phone. "She'll do anything to keep my baby boy away from me."

"Your baby boy is a grown man with a wife and two kids. I'm sure she'd like help putting the kids to bed."

"You wouldn't understand, Eden," she said. "You don't have a family of your own to love and cherish."

"Why would I? I'm too busy avoiding the one I have."

"Don't you start with me, young lady. I'm more than happy to add more money to the murder jar."

Sean squinted. "Did she just say something about a murder jar?"

I covered the phone with my hand. "She said she needs me to look at her scar. She had a mole on her butt biopsied this week." I figured an embarrassing comment about my mother's body would be enough to distract him.

Sure enough, Sean's lip curled. "Hope it's nothing."

"I can't come home right now," I said. "The lightbulb will have to wait until tomorrow."

"But it's dark," my mother complained.

"Then use another light." I shoved my phone back into my pocket. "I guess you're going to deal with the body and I'm going to hunt for the snake?" And the cat.

Sean raked a hand through his hair. "I don't think either one of us gets the better end of the stick."

"Because there is no better end." Only a bitter end for Eloise. "I'm going to search the house for Mischief before I look for the snake." The thought of checking under the beds freaked me out. I didn't want to come face-to-face with a set of fangs.

"Maybe we shouldn't split up," Sean said, looking around anxiously.

I arched an eyebrow. "Why not?"

"It's starting to feel like a horror movie, but instead of a rabid dog, we're dealing with a rabid snake."

"Well, that's impossible because snakes aren't mammals," I said.

Sean's brow creased. "They can't be rabid?"

I groaned in exasperation. "I'd wonder about your education if I hadn't sat next to you in science class."

He adjusted his belt, seemingly to give the appearance of having everything under control. "It's getting late. I'll call the Chief Medical Examiner's Office now."

I tiptoed through the foyer, avoiding the broken glass and the body. "Here, kitty, kitty." I walked slowly through the house and made the whispering sound reserved for cats. I checked in closets and under beds. I even checked inside the kitchen cabinets but no dice. It was time to search outside. I took a flashlight from the junk drawer next to the refrigerator and headed out the back door. It was possible the cat was staying close to the house, but staying hidden.

"Mischief," I called softly. "Come here, girl. You don't want to stay out here with that nasty snake roaming free." I rifled through my purse to see whether I had anything that would tempt a cat. My fingers slid over my wallet, my badge, a packet of tissues, a tampon, and a half-eaten granola bar. Nope. Nothing for Mischief.

Darkness washed over me as I left the house and I switched on the flashlight. I crept along the perimeter of the yard looking for eye shine and listening for the sound of a slithering snake. At this point, the discovery of either one would be a bonus. The scattering of leaves grabbed my attention and I directed the light into the cluster of trees behind the house. A deer stared back at me, its dainty tail flicking back and forth.

"Carry on," I said. "Nothing to see here."

I moved to the bushes along the side of the house and came up empty-handed. There were no streetlights in this neighborhood, so I was glad to have the flashlight. I continued to the neighbor's house and found more snakeskin in Mrs. Langley's yard, but no actual snake and no cat. I proceeded to scan every yard on the block without success. As much as I hated to give up, there was nothing more I could do tonight. I left Sean to handle Eloise and went home to break the sad news to the chief.

I snuck into the house as quietly as I could and hoped that Princess Buttercup didn't alert anyone to my arrival. I tiptoed upstairs to the attic and found Alice hovering protectively over the fox that was curled in a tight ball on my pillow. He raised his head when he saw me.

"I got scared when you weren't in the barn," I said.

"I urged him into the house when I heard your family decide to sneak a peek in the barn," Alice said.

Because of course they did.

"I tried to hold the doors shut to keep them out," Alice said. "Olivia nearly caught her finger and cried, so everyone went back inside."

I frowned. "How did you communicate with Sawyer? He can't see you."

"No, but he's not an idiot. I made sure he felt my presence first and then encouraged him to leave the barn. When I opened the doors for him, he was smart enough to walk through them."

"Thanks, Alice," I said. "Sawyer, I'm afraid I have sad news." I positioned myself beside him on the mattress. "We've lost a local resident, Eloise Worthington." I stroked the fox's soft fur. "You don't have to worry. It wasn't murder. Just the wrong place at the wrong time. Deputy Guthrie is handling it."

The fox looked at me with concern in his dark eyes and I wondered whether it stemmed from the death or the fact that Sean was in charge of handling it.

"I told Sean to text you so that I can answer him and pretend to be you," I said. "Hopefully we won't have to keep this going much longer. Tomorrow morning we're going to test another theory and see if we can bring you back."

"You haven't asked your mother to get involved, have you?" Alice asked.

"Do I look insane to you? There's no magic involved this time, just a werewolf and his indomitable will."

The fox yawned.

"You seem awfully tired for an animal that spent the evening on a mattress," I said.

"We watched television earlier," Alice said. "I thought he might like CHiPs."

I shot him an accusatory look. "More potato chips?"

"No, CHiPs," Alice said. "The show about police officers

on the highways of Los Angeles. They wear uniforms like his."

I burst into laughter. "If he were a cop in the 70's, sure." I smiled at the fox. "I bet he really enjoyed that. Thank you, Alice. You're very considerate."

"He seems lonely."

"Of course he does. He's been transformed into an animal and he can't communicate. It sucks."

"Maybe Clara can read his emotions," Alice suggested.

"That's not a bad idea." I cut a sideways look at the fox. "Except I don't think I need help reading his emotions. He's worried and scared. He wants to figure out what went wrong so we can make it right. I know because I feel the same way."

The fox's nod was almost imperceptible.

The mention of Clara sparked a reminder. "Do you know anything about a secret club for descendants of the original Puritan families?"

"A secret club?" Alice repeated. She drifted over in front of a pile of multi-colored storage containers. "Why would they need a secret club?"

"That's what we're wondering."

The ghost appeared thoughtful. "I'm not aware of any organization that's restricted to descendants of founding families. I would have been a member."

"You wouldn't have been required to join," I said. "Farley Twisse isn't a member, but he could be if he wanted to."

"Do you want me to skulk around town and see what I can find out?" Alice offered.

"Looking after the chief is the priority right now," I said. "Maybe later." And maybe Clara would find something useful in the town archives.

"If a club needs to be hidden, then it probably shouldn't exist in the first place," Alice said.

I had a feeling she was right about this particular organization. It seemed odd to hide its existence in a town that celebrated its founding families with statues and street names. That didn't track.

"Secrets are hard work," Alice continued. "Active deception is exhausting. It causes stress and anxiety…"

"Thanks, Alice. I think we get the idea."

The ghost seemed to realize her error. "Oh, I didn't mean you, Eden."

I leaned against the soft fur of the fox for support. "I know." And the truth was that the stress and anxiety would be worse if my family knew about us. Whatever we endured as a result of hiding the secret was worth it.

Alice gave me a sympathetic look. "Telling the truth is like lighting a torch. It can bring light and clarity."

"Or it can set your house on fire," I finished. And, when it came to my family, I knew which one I could count on.

CHAPTER TWELVE

THE NEXT MORNING I snuck downstairs bright and early to grab food for the fox. I was stunned to see my mother back to her usual, middle-aged self. It all made sense when I heard Grandma speak. Unlike the Go-Go's, her lips were unsealed.

"You're up early," Grandma said. "I didn't hear you come in last night so I assumed you'd sleep until noon."

"When do I ever sleep until noon?" I asked. I debated whether to mention their truce but decided it was best to pretend the fight never happened. That was my family's way —eruption and denial.

My mother spooned sugar into her coffee. "I think we might have mice in the attic. Have you seen any? I keep hearing the sound of scuffling."

My stomach clenched when I realized she'd been hearing the fox walking around on the attic floorboards. "I haven't noticed any, but I'll keep an eye out."

"I'll send Candy up to take care of them," Grandma said, with a nod toward the black cat that was sprawled across the windowsill. Candy opened a lazy eye at the mention of her name.

"No need for that," I said quickly. Although Candy didn't look particularly vicious, the cat could make all your death wishes come true.

Aunt Thora ambled into the kitchen wearing an eyeshade on her head. Apparently she decided to tough it out at the farmhouse last night. "There are muffins in the tin. I made lemon-poppy seed."

"Great, thanks." If my mother and Grandma were smart, they'd behave better for Aunt Thora's sake. If she left, so did the delicious baked goods that everyone inhaled.

"Coffee's in the pot," my mother said. "I know it isn't up to your exacting standards, but it's there."

"Thank you." I had no desire to pick a fight. Now that she and Grandma were out of each other's crosshairs, I'd be a tempting target.

"How was the meeting last night?" my mother asked. "Anything interesting to report?"

"No," I lied. "Just the usual."

"It's been a bit of a lull for you, hasn't it?" Aunt Thora said. "It seemed like demons were climbing out of the woodwork. I guess that's finally calmed down."

"Seems so." I filled a mug to the brim with coffee and inhaled the aroma. It was one of my favorite smells in the world, even when the coffee itself was mediocre. The bright yellow mug read *I am a ray of f$*%ing sunshine* in block cap letters. One of Grandma's.

"I don't recall Paul Pidcock having so much activity," Grandma said. "It must be something you're doing."

My mother glanced at her. "What? You think the demons sent a memo around Otherworld advertising fresh meat in the Chipping Cheddar FBM office?"

Grandma shrugged. "Could be. You don't know."

I joined them at the table. "I highly doubt it." I drank my coffee in contemplative silence. Part of me wanted to launch into a tirade about their spell on Tanner. The other part of me knew it was a fool's errand, at least right now. I couldn't risk riling them up while Chief Fox was in a vulnerable position. He needed me to stay on top of his case and not be sidelined by a hex or worse. It was tough sitting with them and pretending everything was fine though. I'd suppressed the anger I felt toward them in order to keep the peace. At some point my lid would blow. It was inevitable.

Princess Buttercup's low growl told me that my guest had arrived. As casually as I could without raising suspicion, I left the table. The hellhound followed me to the attic steps. "You stay here. Hugh is here to do me a favor and I don't need you spewing the flames of the underworld at him. It's rude."

I ran upstairs and scooped up the fox, tucking him under my shirt to keep him out of sight in case I passed any family members on the way out. His fur tickled the bare skin of my stomach and I suppressed a giggle.

"Do you think your family won't notice that huge bulge under your shirt?" Alice asked, drifting next to me.

"I'll just tell them I'm pregnant," I said. "That'll distract them long enough for me to escape."

"I think you're safe if you hurry," Alice said. "Your mother and grandmother are still at the table."

I held my breath and walked downstairs on the tips of my toes, then slipped out the back door. I set the fox on the ground and we ran to the barn where Hugh awaited us. His hair was unkempt and his clothes slightly disheveled. He wasn't kidding about not being an early riser.

I opened the doors to the barn. "Watch out for the tools and tarps. John's almost finished and I don't want anything to slow him down."

Hugh gave the room an admiring glance. "This room is going to be quite the feature."

"I don't know how you can tell. John's taken great pains

to hide everything so he can do a big reveal." He'd been inspired by all those HGTV shows. "I'm not allowed anywhere in the barn except this room."

"I was thinking about converting an outbuilding on my property. I'd like a man cave." He knocked on a wooden post on the wall. "I definitely think I'll hire him. This transformation is remarkable."

"It is," I agreed. "And I'm counting down the minutes until I can move in."

"Feel free to call me to keep you company if you get lonely."

I pointed in the direction of the farmhouse. "You do realize that I can't throw a stone without hitting a member of my family, right? There's no such thing as lonely for me."

"I think my wife misses her homeland," Hugh said with a tragic sigh. "I fear it might have been a mistake to bring her here."

"Gee, imagine my shock that a mail order werewolf bride isn't living the dream."

Hugh rolled up his sleeves. "Let's get down to business, shall we? I have a busy day today and sarcasm isn't on the agenda."

"Hey, the sooner the chief is back in his physical form, the better for everyone."

Hugh clucked his tongue as he regarded the fox. "A dull brown coat. Too bad you didn't get anything flashier to attract female attention."

"I don't think the chief is concerned about attracting foxy ladies," I said.

Hugh shrugged. "He might want to consider it if this is a new normal for him."

I resisted the urge to punch Hugh in the Adam's apple. "This is not a new normal," I insisted. "Even if he is a kitsune or some kind of shifter, it doesn't mean he'll want to use his abilities."

Hugh grunted his disagreement. "You're the anomaly, Eden, not the norm. Most of us are comfortable with who we are. We actually like our supernatural selves."

I bristled. "I like myself."

Hugh snorted. "Whatever." He moved into a crouched position to address the fox. "Listen up, Chief Fox. I'm a were-wolf, in case you haven't worked that out yet. I'm going to walk you through how to shift. When I've finished, you can try. Simple, right?"

I glanced at the fox to see whether he understood. Based on his earlier responses, he seemed to be following the conversation without any trouble.

Hugh started to strip off his clothes. He'd made it as far as his black boxer briefs when I threw out my hands. "Whoa! Slow down there, partner. I don't think we need the full show."

Hugh grinned. "Honey, everybody needs a glimpse of this package."

The fox lowered himself to the ground and covered his eyes with his paws.

"You're here to help him shift, not strip," I said, trying not to sound impatient.

Hugh stood in his briefs and socks and faced the fox. "I'm not sure if it'll be exactly the same for you, but you should feel a special kind of energy in the pit of your stomach. Something that doesn't quite belong, yet also feels absolutely right."

I rolled my eyes. "That's crystal clear, Hugh. You should consider teaching a class."

The werewolf ignored me. "Then you focus on that energy and start pulling on it. You want it to open like a flower in your gut."

I winced. Now there was a lovely image.

"The animal is coiled in there like a snake, and you're going to let it loose," Hugh continued.

I gestured to the fox. "He's already let it loose, Hugh. That's why we're here. How does he put the furry genie back in the bottle?"

Hugh rubbed his hands together. "That's what I'm attempting to demonstrate."

"Tell me again why you needed to strip for this demonstration?" I asked.

Hugh leered at me. "Thought you might want to show me the bedroom afterward."

The fox snarled.

"I thought you were only into werewolves," I said. "What's with the sudden onslaught of smarminess?"

"For marriage and progeny purposes, yes," Hugh said. "Now that I have my bride, I'm open to other arrangements." He inclined his head toward the fox. "I don't see why the chief should object. We're two willing adults."

"Make that one willing adult. I'm not interested." I motioned to the pile of clothes. "You might as well get dressed."

"I intended to shift to wolf form and then back again." Hugh grabbed his shirt and pulled it down over his head. "But, honestly, I don't think I'm what he needs."

"How can you tell?" I asked, suddenly filled with desperation. "He hasn't shifted yet."

"Exactly my point. If he were a shifter, we'd see an arm or a leg by now. Some evidence that he can transform at will. Whatever's happened to him, I'm afraid his will has nothing to do with it."

"What in the devil is going on in here?"

My body jolted at the sound of Grandma's voice.

"Good morning, Mrs. Pritchard," Hugh said warmly.

"Why are you getting naked in the barn with Eden?" Her gaze flicked to the fox. "Is this some kind of weird threesome?"

"No, Grandma. You don't understand."

Grandma crossed her arms. "I understand kink when I see it."

My mother appeared behind her. "You should at least get another shifter involved. A random fox from the woods could be riddled with disease."

Inwardly I groaned. Leave it to my mother to offer threesome tips.

"You sound like you have experience in these matters, Mrs. Fury," Hugh said.

My mother's eyelashes fluttered. "Please, call me Beatrice. All the men do."

"That's not all they call you," Grandma muttered. She moved toward the fox and swatted at him. "Get out of here before we all get rabies."

I rushed between them. "Leave him alone."

"Oh, how sweet. Eden's already become attached," my mother said. "Sweetheart, you can have a physical relationship without getting emotionally involved. Trust me, I do it all the time."

An involuntary shudder escaped me. "There are so many things wrong with that sentence that I don't know where to start."

Hugh zipped his pants and slipped on his shoes. "The barn suddenly feels a bit crowded. I think I'll be going. Sorry I couldn't be more help."

My mother made a sad face. "Oh, could you not manage?"

"He managed fine." I maneuvered in front of Hugh before he registered the offensive remark.

"What does Eden need help with in the barn?" Grandma asked. "She has John for the carpentry work."

"Not the barn," Hugh said. "The fox."

No. No. No. "Thanks, Hugh. See you later."

Grandma and my mother looked at the fox in question. "What's wrong with the fox?" Grandma asked. "Looks healthy to me."

"Yes, but the chief would like to resume his human form," Hugh said.

I wanted to throttle the werewolf.

"The chief?" my mother echoed. "That fox is the chief?"

"He's been stuck in fox form for days," Hugh said. "Eden asked for my help in getting him to shift back."

"Since when is he a shifter?" my mother asked.

"He's not," Hugh said. "At least I don't think that's what we're dealing with."

Grandma bent over to examine the fox and looked directly into his eyes. "He's aware of everything that's happening."

"I know," I said.

"How can you be sure?" my mother asked.

"Because I've basically been with him since he turned," I said. "He's been staying with me in the attic so that I could make sure he was safe until he returned to normal."

My mother's cheeks were tinged with pink. "He's been staying in the attic under our very roof and you didn't tell us?"

"Oops, I can see I've stirred the cauldron on this one. Good luck, Eden." Hugh slipped out from behind me and clapped me on the back before making his way to the exit.

Princess Buttercup passed Hugh on her way into the barn. She must've heard the commotion and come to check things out. She sniffed the floor where Hugh's clothes had been and then sprawled across the middle of the room.

"This is unbelievable," my mother complained. "Did you

really think you could keep a secret from me, Eden Joy Fury?"

Wow. The middle name too. "I've kept a lot of secrets from you over the years," I shot back. "You didn't know about Tanner until Anton blabbed."

I could practically see the steam ready to blow from my mother's ears. "And what does this have to do with that wretched human boyfriend of yours?"

"Because that fox is also a wretched human," I said. "No, wait. Just a human, not a wretched one." I was careful to omit the word 'boyfriend.'

"Why is he your responsibility?" Grandma asked.

"Because supernatural occurrences in this town are my responsibility. I can't very well hand him over to Deputy Guthrie."

"What about the supernatural council?" my mother asked. "Or is that why Hugh was here?" She glanced at the doorway where Hugh had disappeared. "I can't say I'd mind if he came back for another striptease."

Grandma snapped her fingers in front of my mother's face. "Leash your inner harlot, Beatrice. We have a situation."

"We do," I admitted. "We need to turn the chief back into a human. Can you help?"

My mother folded her arms and glared at me. "No."

I balked. "No?"

"You heard me. You keep secrets from me and this is what happens. I hope you've learned a valuable lesson."

"Mom, you're not punishing me. You're punishing the chief of police and the residents of Chipping Cheddar."

"I'm punishing you by not doing what you want," my mother said. "His disappointment is simply a byproduct."

"Watch this!" Grandma's eyes glinted with mischief.

I watched in horror as she gestured to the fox and

snapped her fingers. The fox ran and did a flying leap over Princess Buttercup. "What are you doing?"

"Isn't it obvious? The quick brown fox jumps over the lazy dog." Grandma cackled softly.

The hellhound lifted her head as if to challenge the accusation of laziness.

"Why is this necessary?" I demanded.

"It's a pangram," Grandma said. "It contains all the letters of the alphabet."

"No, but why are you turning the chief into a dog and pony...fox show?" I asked.

"I used a little puppet magic to control his movements," Grandma said. "No big deal."

"Please don't do that to the chief of police," I said. "If you're going to do anything, give him the ability to speak so he can communicate." That was better than nothing.

My mother and Grandma exchanged looks. "Fine," my mother said. "You can owe us one." She glanced at Grandma. "You should probably do it. My body is still recovering from your dreadful hex."

Grandma mimicked my mother's voice as she drew blood from her palm with a sharp fingernail. "Open your gullet, fox," she demanded.

The fox reluctantly opened his mouth and Grandma dripped blood into it while chanting in Latin. Then she flicked her fingers at the fox.

"Finally! Do you know how long I've been wanting to speak?"

My spirits soared at the sound of the chief's voice. I longed to kiss his snout, but I had to control myself. With my family present, that kind of response was impossible.

"You can thank us later for restoring your power of speech," my mother said.

"How about restoring my arms and legs?" Chief Fox asked.

"No can do," my mother said.

"I heard what you told Eden," he said. "You can. You just won't."

My mother heaved a sigh. "That was a lie. We can't do it. Being able to communicate with you is the best we can do."

My head jerked toward her. "What? You can't use your dark…" I stumbled over my words, not wanting to say too much in front of the chief. "Your dark blue magic pouch?"

"Afraid not," Grandma said. "Our options are limited."

"How do you know if you don't try?" I demanded.

"Eden, I don't think you want us to do anything more… potent in the chief's presence," my mother said under her breath. "It's bad enough he's been exposed to our true natures at all."

She was right. It was one thing for the chief to know they were witches. It was quite another if he witnessed one of their more powerful spells. It was hard to hide that their brand of magic was dark.

I focused on the fox. "What do you remember?"

He angled his head toward my family. "I don't think you want me to divulge too many details."

"Of course we do," my mother said. "How else can we figure out what happened to you?"

"I was…with a friend," he said. "One minute we were having a great time and, the next minute, I was a fox."

"Where were you when this happened?" my mother asked.

"In my house," the chief replied.

"What were you doing?" Grandma asked. "Watching television? Playing Little Critters?"

"What's Little Critters?" the chief asked.

I waved him off. "It's not important."

126

"I wasn't doing anything that would turn me into a fox," he said.

My mother popped a hand on her hip. "Well, you must've done something or this wouldn't have happened," she said.

"You're blaming the victim now?" Chief Fox asked. "Fine, if you must know, we'd just locked lips."

My mother smiled. "Ooh, do tell. How was it?"

"Very nice. I'd definitely do it again if I get the chance." I could've sworn the fox was smiling.

"I didn't realize you had that kind of friend in town," Grandma said.

"Because the chief's personal life isn't our business," I said quickly.

"How did you know this happened, Eden?" Aunt Thora asked.

"His friend called me," I said. "They know what I do and figured I could help."

Grandma crossed her arms. "Being a fox is the least of his problems."

I looked at her. "How so?"

"Now he knows about us," she said. "We have to kill him."

"No, we have to *help* him," I said.

"I don't recommend planning my murder when I can hear you," the fox said.

Grandma shrugged. "Who cares? You'll be dead."

"What about a demon?" my mother asked. "Isn't that your job, Eden—to figure out this stuff?"

I stifled a frustrated groan. "Neville and I have been doing the research, but we haven't come up with a plausible option. I thought a shifter was a possibility."

"Apparently not," Grandma said.

"The LeRoux witches couldn't undo the spell either," the chief said.

My mother and Grandma exchanged looks. "I'm sorry,"

Grandma said. "I think I misheard you because you're a fox. Did you say the LeRoux witches tried to break the spell on you?"

"Yes," the chief said.

I pressed my lips together. I was going to pay for that revelation. "I had to ask Adele first. She's on the council."

My mother smiled. "And clearly that was an exercise in futility because he's still a fox."

"What do we do now?" Chief Fox asked.

I pulled my phone from my pocket. "Now that you can speak, I think we should call Deputy Guthrie and let him know you're alive. I think he was starting to doubt me."

The fox directed his attention to my mother and Grandma. "Would it be possible to have privacy? I'm about to conduct official police business on speakerphone."

"Yes, Chief Fox," my mother said. "We understand."

"And please don't reveal my condition to anyone," he said. "We can't afford to have panic in the streets."

"I highly doubt that would happen," Grandma said. "There are other ways of keeping the peace besides a human in uniform."

"No matter how attractive he looks in it," my mother added.

Ew. It was bad enough to have my mother hitting on my boyfriend, but to do it while he was in his fox form? Ick.

I clicked on Sean's number and put him on speaker. I listened to the chief fake a cough and reassure the deputy that he'd be better soon. Sean seemed to buy it. He told the chief all about Eloise and the snake.

"You've got it covered, Guthrie," the chief said. "I trust you."

"Thank you, sir." I could practically hear Sean beaming through the phone. "If I may ask, why are you calling me from Eden's phone?"

"Mine ran out of juice," the chief said. "She came by to deliver a report and I asked to use hers."

"Goodbye, Sean," I called. I clicked off the phone and put it away. "That went well enough."

"For now," the chief said. "Eventually, he'll want to see me."

"We'll figure it out." We had to.

"The barn looks great from what I can see, by the way," he said. "I look forward to spending time here. In my human form, of course."

"Gods, I really hope so," I said.

The fox looked at me expectantly. "Which part?"

I offered a shaky smile. "Both." But I was beginning to worry that, soon enough, one of those would no longer be an option.

CHAPTER THIRTEEN

"I CAN'T BELIEVE I've never been in here before," I said. I stood inside Treasure Trove and ogled the gorgeous interior. Gilded mirrors, chandeliers, a gleaming piano. It was like walking into a Newport mansion.

"I can't believe you haven't either," Neville said. "It's wonderful. You've been missing out."

"There were antique stores in San Francisco that I used to browse in," I said. "It was one of my favorite things to do when I wasn't working."

Neville cocked an eyebrow. "There were times you weren't working, Agent Fury? Do tell."

"Did someone say Fury?" A slender man emerged from behind a large armoire. "Oh, hello, Neville. I thought I recognized one of the voices out here."

"Hello, Foster," Neville said. "I'd like you to meet my boss, Agent Eden Fury."

Foster looked me up and down. "Yes, of course. I see the resemblance to Moyer."

"You can thank him for the recommendation that I come here. I didn't realize this place was here."

Foster leaned against the armoire. "Are you looking for a particular item? I understand you have a renovated barn to furnish. We could do wonders for that here."

I felt a prickle of excitement at the thought of decorating my new home. "That's a definite yes. Unfortunately, I'll have to focus on that another time. Right now, I need to know if you have any items that would lend themselves to transmorphication."

Foster didn't bat an eye at the mention of a magical term. "You want to change someone into something else? I hope this isn't to settle a family dispute. I know your people play hardball." He chuckled.

"As enticing as the prospect is, no," I said. "I can't really say more than that. This is a confidential investigation."

Foster swiveled, his gaze sweeping the shop. "I don't believe I have anything in stock that would support a spell like that."

"Have you sold any items recently that would have?" I asked. "Anything at all?"

"Nothing that connects to a spell like that," Foster said. "A wingback chair. A pedestal table." He mentally walked through his recent sales. "No, nothing springs to mind."

"Do you have a book section?" I asked.

"I know where that is," Neville said.

Foster smiled. "You certainly do. One of my best customers, apart from Moyer. If it's written in an ancient language, Moyer is my first call. I don't even bother to translate the titles."

Neville led me to a single step that emptied into another, smaller room. Two walls were lined with bookshelves. The scent of leather hit me as I approached the first section.

"How are they organized?" I asked.

"The middle section is our best bet," Neville said.

I stared at the dozens of spines. "But if there's a book

here, how does that help us? Wouldn't the culprit have taken the book?"

"If they were smart, they would have read it here and not bought it," Neville said. "That way, it can't be traced back to them."

I clapped my assistant on the shoulder. "Sometimes your brain is worth its weight in gold."

Neville's cheeks colored. "It *is* rather on the heavy side."

I contemplated the rows of books. "Can you do a spell to see which books were most recently handled? Some kind of trace?"

Neville brightened. "Indeed, I can."

"Do you have what you need?" I asked.

Neville unhooked his backpack from his shoulder. "While I always try to come prepared, I might need a thing or two more to complete this particular spell." He glanced around the room. "Ah, right. There are a few items I can use in the front room. I'll be right back."

I strolled in front of the shelves, resisting the urge to tug books from their places while I waited for Neville to return. I didn't want to interfere with the results.

He hurried back into the room and I noticed a wooden elevated cake stand. "It's perfect. It's made of acacia."

"Are we presenting a cake at the end of the spell?" I asked.

"I need a stand made of a natural material for the candle," he said. "It helps channel the magic. You can't use anything synthetic or the spell won't work properly."

I gestured to the floor. "Apologies, Magical Martha Stewart. Carry on."

Neville crouched down and pulled a candle and a packet of matches from his backpack, along with a sealed bag of herbs.

"Foster won't mind that we're about to light up in his shop?" I asked.

"No," he said. "If any customers come in, Foster said he'll keep them occupied in the other room until we're finished."

"He's a real hidden gem, isn't he?" It was a pleasure to meet someone intent on helping rather than hindering.

"That's one of the perks of being an introvert," Neville said. "You get to know all the best people by sitting quietly and listening."

"I'll keep a lookout in case Foster gets preoccupied with a customer," I said. While the wizard performed the spell, I wandered in and around the furniture stock, mentally placing my favorite items in the barn. There was the loveseat that Sawyer and I would use to snuggle under a blanket on chilly nights. There was the dining table that we'd use to eat our breakfast before heading off to work—together, of course. He'd drop me off at the office and then...

"O wondrous infernal goddess?" Neville called.

I snapped out of my fantasy world where Sawyer and I apparently lived our lives like a Hallmark couple and hurried back to my assistant. "Any luck?"

"Afraid not. The only books recently handled are *The Many, Many Letters of Alexander Hamilton* and *The Joy of Ancient Sex.*"

I cringed. "Is that ancient sexual customs or sex with old people?"

"I opted not to investigate any further."

"Smart man."

"How's it going in here?" Foster sauntered into the room.

"Unfortunately, we didn't find what we're looking for," I replied.

"We did, however, find a book called *All About Muffs,*" Neville announced.

I swiveled to gape at him. "Excuse me?"

He wore an innocent expression. "What? They kept women's hands warm in the colder months."

I balked. "And I ask again—what?"

"The book is all about women's fashions in Colonial America," Neville said. "A fascinating read."

"I'll take your word for it," I said.

"Have you tried the used bookstore yet?" Foster asked. "Perhaps they have what you're looking for."

"Thanks, that's our next stop," I said.

"I'm sorry I couldn't be more help," Foster said, as we headed toward the exit.

"If you don't mind me asking, how old were you when you realized you had the Sight?"

Foster smiled. "Too young. My parents thought I was bonkers, although they started telling people that I had a vivid imagination to make me look sane. They weren't very understanding."

"Did you grow up here?" I asked.

"No," Foster said. "I came here on a trip one summer and felt a certain level of comfort. It was only when I met Moyer that I realized why."

"You knew what he was?" I asked.

"I knew he was Other." Foster straightened a trio of candlesticks. "I knew I was Other, too. I just didn't realize how normal I was in comparison until I was introduced to more supers." He laughed. "If only my parents knew."

"You didn't tell them?" I asked.

He bowed his head. "They died long before then. I think they'd be pleased to know that I found my place in the world though. Childhood is rough for kids like me. There's so much confusion. Maybe if I'd grown up here where it's more accepted…"

"I'm glad you're happy here." It was ironic in a way. Foster had found greener pastures in the very place I'd left—in search of greener pastures.

"I'm quite content," he replied. "And the town was in dire need of a quality antiques shop. The other options are adequate, but they're more for tourists, full of knick knacks and other tchotchkes."

"You do have beautiful items in here," I said. Everywhere I turned, I saw an item of interest. A turn of the century green trunk with black wood trim and brass detailing. A small mahogany drum table. A walnut grandfather clock. Best of all, no creepy dolls.

"Be sure to come back when it's time to decorate that beautiful barn," Foster said.

"I promise."

Neville and I left the shop and the smell of curry burned my nostrils.

"Are you ready for lunch, Agent Fury?" Neville asked.

"I'd rather hit the bookstore first," I said. "I'm feeling too anxious to eat. You go ahead though. I'll let you know if I find anything."

"You can't perform the trace spell without me," he said.

"I don't know that I need to do one. It depends."

Neville's stomach rumbled and he laughed, his cheeks tinged with pink. "Oops. I guess I should make eating a priority."

I clapped him on the back. "Catch up with me when you're done."

"I'll take Achilles for a walk as well. Let me stretch those tiny legs."

"Good idea." We parted ways at the corner and I carried on walking to Barely Buzzed Books. The shop was a newer addition to town and took over the original bookshop after I left for college. According to Grandma, it was owned by a 'dirty hippie who hasn't seen a haircut since 1979' and she refused to step foot in there. Grandma also vented about the fact that the shop served tea but not coffee, as though coffee was a requirement for book browsing.

A bell rang as I opened the door and the woman behind the counter offered a friendly smile. She was short and stout with cropped brown hair and perfectly square teeth. So much for a dirty hippie.

"Welcome. My name is Penelope. Let me know if you need help finding anything."

I scanned the interior. It had a homey feel, with garden furniture that functioned as seating and stacks of books that looked more like someone's home library than a shop. I glanced at the floor and realized I was standing on an area rug with the design of a pentagram. The design was nearly lost amidst a riot of colors.

"Expecting any evil spirits?" I joked, and pointed to the rug.

Penelope followed my finger. "Oh, I just like the rug. I found it in the antique store here for my house, but it didn't suit my living room so I brought it here instead."

"It looks like it belongs," I said.

"Thank you. Can I offer you any tea? I have a nettle tea with mint that's sublime."

"I'm good, thanks." I approached the counter. "I'm doing an online university class and I need to do research on the weirdest topic." I laughed awkwardly. "Transmorphication. Have you ever heard of such a thing?"

The woman's brow furrowed. "No, but it sounds interesting. What is it?"

"Changing one thing into another," I said vaguely.

"Like water into ice?" she asked.

I hesitated. "Less science and more pseudoscience."

"You're taking a pseudoscience class? Awesome. Does it cover telepathy and astral projection?"

"Not quite. Can you tell me if you have any books on the subject?"

Penelope turned to her computer. "Let me take a look for you." She typed on the keyboard and peered at the results. "Nothing under that term. Is there another one I should try?"

"Animal transformation."

Penelope smiled. "Like werewolves?"

"Yes," I said, without further explanation.

Penelope clicked the keys and squinted. "How about that? We have a few options. Well, sort of."

I leaned over the counter, trying to see the screen. "What does that mean?"

"It means the book includes the topic but isn't dedicated to it. Like maybe there's a chapter on it or something. If it's mentioned in the index or the Table of Contents, it'll show up in the results."

Perfect. "If you could point me in their direction, that would be great."

"I can point you to two of them. Another one was purchased recently and we only had one copy, so I'm afraid you're out of luck."

On the contrary. "What's the name of the book?"

"The one that was purchased?" I nodded and she reviewed the screen. "*Spells and Enchantments for the Beginner*." She laughed. "I remember that one. The cover was so pretty. I think that's the main reason I ordered it for the store."

"I know this is a strange request, but would you mind telling me the name of the person who bought the book?"

Penelope hesitated. "I don't think I can do that. It would violate their privacy."

I dug around my purse and produced my badge. To humans without the Sight, it read FBI.

Penelope's eyes widened. "I'm so sorry. I didn't realize."

"I'm investigating cyber fraud," I said. "It would be helpful to have that name."

For a moment, I worried that Penelope would demand a warrant, but she turned back to the screen in a tizzy. "Yes, absolutely. You can count on me, ma'am."

"Agent Fury," I said.

Penelope hit a button and the printer came to life. "Her name is Rhonda Milliken."

Hmm. That name wasn't familiar and Milliken wasn't a name of any of the town founders. "Thanks. Any chance I can get an address?"

"It's on the printout," she said, and handed me the sheet of paper.

"This is really helpful. Thank you so much."

"Feel free to come back anytime. On Tuesdays we host a trivia night and Thursdays are open mic. Sometimes we host a poetry slam."

"That sounds fun." Sort of.

"I try to make this place more than a bookstore. I want it to be a spot for the community to gather, like the old mill used to be. I also rent out the lower floor to organizations for their meetings. A lot of book clubs like to use it."

"There's a lower floor?"

She gave me a sheepish grin. "Technically it's the basement, but nobody likes to say they hold their meetings in a basement. It's set up real nice with couches and a big coffee table. If you're interested, I can give you a tour. It's not a huge space, so it won't take long."

"Maybe another time," I said. Now that I had a lead, I didn't want to get distracted.

"Just make a note that you can't have a group with more than twenty-five people because of fire safety regulations. I have a group that meets once a month and they're at the max. I told them they can't add anyone new or they'll have to meet somewhere else. Apparently they used to meet at the library, but they wanted to move to a private space."

"Wow, that sounds like a good group if they can attract that many people on a regular basis. What kind of books do they read?"

"History, apparently," Penelope said. "That's all I know. They're funny about sharing information." She laughed it off. "I don't see what's so embarrassing about history books. You'd think they were down there watching porn."

"Let's hope not or I might have to make an appearance," I teased, wiggling my badge.

Penelope covered her mouth. "Oh, my. I can just imagine the look on Joan Worland's face if you accused her of watching porn with a group of old men."

My radar pinged. "Joan Worland? She's in this book club?"

"Yes, do you know her? I suppose you would. She's a fixture in this town, isn't she? Come to think of it, lots of them are fixtures."

"Who else?" I asked. I had a feeling I already knew the answers, or some of them anyway.

Penelope pursed her lips, thinking. "Patrick Smallwood, Oliver Sewall, Yolanda Lloyd, Grier Hatton. I don't have a list of names, but those are the ones I've noticed heading down there. I leave Patrick a key and he locks up when they're done."

"That's very trusting of you," I said.

She shrugged. "He's a small business owner. Actually, most of them are. It's something they have in common."

That wasn't the only thing they had in common. Every name she mentioned was also a descendant of a founding family. "When's their next meeting? I know I can't join unless someone drops out, but maybe there's a waiting list I can be added to."

"You'll have to talk to Patrick or Joan about that," Penelope said. "They meet on the third Friday night of every month."

"Thanks." I tucked the paper with Rhonda's address into my purse. "You've been more helpful than you know."

CHAPTER FOURTEEN

I GOT in my car and texted Clara the information I'd learned about the monthly 'book club' meetings. I had a strong feeling that the only history books they read were the ones that included their families' names.

Clara texted back immediately. *Thanks! Want to spy with me at the next meeting?*

I thought about the invisibility charm that Neville had made for me. *Absolutely.* Even though it wasn't for another three weeks, I added the date to the calendar on my phone.

I sent another text to Neville to let him know that I was following up on a lead. He sent back a Caucasian thumbs up emoji and a dog emoji. I was glad to see that he was enjoying his time with Achilles. It would be hard not to though. The pug was undeniably sweet.

I drove to the house on Burrata Street. It was a classic colonial-style family home with a symmetrical facade and a brass knocker on the front door. The doormat was personalized with *Welcome to the Millikens*. Although I felt guilty standing on their name, there was nowhere else to put my feet. There was a car in the driveway, so I crossed my fingers that Rhonda was home. I rang the doorbell and waited.

I only had to wait about ten seconds for the door to open a crack. A middle-aged woman was partially visible. With rosy cheeks and a soft body, she was what my father would describe as 'pleasantly plump.' Of course he would then go a step further and say that she'd be pretty if she lost twenty pounds, prompting Anton and I to chastise him for his insensitive remark. He'd act like we were being ridiculous and accuse our generation of being 'too soft.' Even in an imaginary conversation, my father managed to irritate me.

"Hi. Are you Rhonda Milliken?" I asked.

The woman seemed slightly taken off-guard. "I am. Is there something I can help you with?"

"My name is Eden Fury. I understand you purchased a book earlier this week," I said.

She frowned. "A book?"

"It's called *Spells and Enchantments for the Beginner*," I said.

She shook her head. "I haven't bought any books since I moved here, and I certainly wouldn't buy one with that title."

"Is it possible that someone stole your credit card?" I retrieved the paper from my purse. "The one that ends in 6524?"

"Hold on and I'll check," she said. She opened the door wider. "Would you like to come in?"

I wiped my feet and stepped into the foyer.

"Apologies for the boxes, but it's taking me forever to unpack."

"Did you move locally?" I asked. I followed her into the bright white kitchen. "I love your subway tiles." The back-splash was comprised of dark grey herringbone tiles that were in stark contrast to the white cabinets. It was wonderfully dramatic.

"Thank you. I wish I could claim responsibility, but the

kitchen was like this when we moved in." She rooted through her purse and pulled out her wallet. She snapped it open and smiled with relief. "The credit card is right here. I guess it's possible someone could've used the number without the card. Which bookstore? I should probably give them a call."

"Is there no one else with access to the card?" I asked. She'd said 'we moved in.' "What about your husband?"

"He has his own AmEx," she said. "It's possible my daughter used it. She's been going into town after school on her own."

"How old is your daughter?" I asked.

"Ava is sixteen," Rhonda replied. "She knows better than to take the card without asking, but she's been known to break the rules more than I'd like." She smiled as if to say 'typical teen,' but my mind was still stuck on the name.

"Ava?" I repeated. The image of the teenager with the oversized glasses flashed in my mind.

"Yes, that's right. She's just started the high school as a junior."

"I've met her. She's friends with Meg, my cousin."

Rhonda broke into a wide smile. "Yes, of course. Meg is wonderful. Ava's been so much happier since she made a friend. The teen years can be so challenging."

"Ava mentioned that you moved for her father's work."

"Yes," she said, but something in her expression told me there was more to the story. "It's not an ideal time to move. I know it would be easier on Ava if we stayed in one place, but it isn't always possible."

"What time does Ava get home from school?" I asked.

Rhonda appeared thoughtful. "She doesn't have any after-school activities today, so around three o'clock."

"Hmm. I'm short on time and I can really use that book. Is there any chance I could look for it now?"

Rhonda bit her lip, seemingly uncertain. "Is there only

one copy in existence? Not to be rude, but why is her particular book so important?"

How could I say more without saying too much? "I'd like to know what Ava intends to do with a book like that."

Rhonda barked a short laugh. "Not much. It's something about enchantments for Pete's sake. What do you think she's going to do? Cast a spell?" She laughed dismissively.

"Okay, I was hoping it wouldn't come to this," I said, and produced my badge.

She gasped. "FBI. Why on earth would you need Ava's book?"

"It's not really about the book," I lied. "I have reason to believe she's storing something inside it." Ugh. I hated to do this to Ava, but time was of the essence. If she was responsible for the chief's condition, I couldn't risk her getting to the book first and destroying evidence. I'd fix the situation with Ava's family later.

Rhonda pressed her hand to her chest. "Is it drugs? Please tell me it's not drugs." She moaned. "I knew trouble would find us again. This always happens. If we could just make it to college…"

Again? "What do you mean?"

Rhonda splayed her hands on the gleaming marble countertop. "That's the real reason we keep moving," she admitted. "No matter where we go, there seems to be trouble. My family blames me, of course."

"Blames you for what?" Could Rhonda be involved somehow?

"They warned me not to adopt a child. That they always come with unknown baggage, but my husband and I couldn't have a child of our own and we really wanted to be parents."

"People come with all sorts of baggage," I said. "Adopted or not."

Tears welled in Rhonda's eyes. "I'm so sorry. That must sound awful. I don't mean to suggest we don't love Ava. We love her beyond all reason."

"You don't have to explain yourself to me," I said. "I understand. Family is complicated." I knew that better than anyone.

"Is she in trouble?" Rhonda asked.

"I'll let you know once I've seen the book."

Rhonda crooked a finger. "Follow me." She took me to a door. "She spends her free time in the basement. My husband and I don't go down there. We try to respect her privacy, especially at this age."

"That's commendable."

"I'm not so sure. Maybe if I had stricter rules, we wouldn't keep having problems."

I lingered at the top of the steps. "What kind of problems do you mean?"

Rhonda licked her lips, appearing to debate how much to reveal. "How about a cup of coffee? I have gingerbread cookies too. They're Ava's favorite."

"Sounds nice," I said. The more I could learn about Ava, the better. I began to worry that Meg might have befriended the wrong sort of girl. She usually had better radar when it came to people.

We returned to the kitchen and Rhonda added a fresh filter and grounds to the coffee pot. She switched on the button. "We left our last town because of a fire."

My heart began to race. "You think Ava started it?"

"She swears she didn't. No one was hurt, fortunately. Our kitchen was toast, but the insurance covered it."

"Why move then?" I asked.

"Because people started to talk." She heaved a sigh. "They always talk."

"What did they say?"

"That Ava started it so that she could murder us and take our money. All kinds of horrible accusations. We knew none of it was true, but once those rumors take off, it's almost impossible to stop them. It impacted her grades and social network. It was awful."

I didn't argue with that. My family had been the subject of many unkind rumors when I was in school. Of course, in my case, the truth was much, much worse.

"When my husband accepted the job in Baltimore, I tried to encourage Ava to move to a city. We could hide better in a busy place, but when we came here, she said she felt more at home than she ever did before. I took it as a sign."

A sign that Ava was likely supernatural. She was probably drawn to the supernatural energy here. "What other issues have you had?"

Rhonda filled two mugs with coffee. "Cream and sugar?"

"Yes, thanks."

She spooned in sugar and stirred. "The town before that there was an incident with some kids at school." She stopped with one hand on the refrigerator door and squeezed her eyes closed for a moment.

"What kind of incident? Was anyone hurt?" I prompted. I was five seconds away from texting Meg to stay far away from Ava Milliken.

She pulled open the door and retrieved the cream. "Only their pride. There was a group of boys who'd apparently been picking on Ava, calling her names. She didn't tell us until after the incident." Rhonda crossed the kitchen and poured cream into both mugs. She handed one to me. "There were three boys involved. They all lost their hair."

"*Lost* their hair?"

Rhonda took a sip of coffee. "They woke up one morning

and they were all bald. Not shaved. Not bleached. Not Just…gone."

"And they blamed Ava?"

"Not just the boys. The school expelled her," Rhonda said. "They said they couldn't prove it, but that Ava had to have been involved given the situation."

"That's not right," I said. "They had no evidence."

"We considered hiring a lawyer, but decided that the damage was done, so we decided to move. Ava didn't want to stay and she's our priority."

"What do you think happened?" I asked. I sucked down a mouthful of coffee. Would it be rude to remind her about the promise of gingerbread cookies? Probably.

"I honestly don't know. My husband and I discussed the possibility that the boys had done it to themselves and blamed Ava to further torment her."

"Why did they pick on her?"

"Why do kids ever pick on each other?" Rhonda asked. "She seemed different to them. Nobody likes different at that age. I still remember being teased for being overweight in fifth grade. It was a horrible time. The school nurse would weigh us and I'd hear the kids behind me in line making jokes about sinking the boat and whale watching." Her eyes brimmed with unshed tears. "People say it's just kids being kids, but that doesn't make it okay. We need to teach our kids compassion and kindness."

I didn't disagree. "If it's any consolation, Mrs. Milliken, kids can grow up to be better people. I've seen it happen." Sassy had been quick with a putdown and happy to make others feel inferior in high school, but she wasn't that girl anymore.

"I was never like that and neither was Ava," Rhonda said. "She's a sweet girl. I'll hate it if she's gotten mixed up in drugs at this point. I would've thought she would've already been through that phase."

I felt terrible for misleading Rhonda, but it was too late now. I just had to press ahead and find the book, as well as any other secrets Ava might be hiding.

"I'm sorry you've had to deal with all that," I said. "It sounds like it's been rough for Ava." I never would've guessed.

"She's settled in nicely here," Rhonda said. "I'd really like to make this work. My husband's lucky he has marketable skills." She frowned. "If you find any drugs in the basement, what happens next?"

"Let's cross that bridge when we come to it, okay?" Because there was no way I'd find drugs in the basement. Herbs for spells maybe, but no drugs. I took another sip of coffee and left the mug on the counter. Knowing me, I'd spill it all over the basement carpet so probably best to leave it upstairs.

I flicked on the light switch and continued down the steps. The first thing I noticed when I reached the bottom was a framed poster of *Wicked* on the wall. So Ava liked musicals about witches and fairies. Nice.

On one side of the room was a pool table and a dartboard on the wall. Across the room was a loveseat and a recliner facing a large flat screen TV affixed to the wall. It was only when I maneuvered past the loveseat that I saw the altar. The book rested on top, as well as a candle and a few other small objects.

Like a pocket watch.

I dropped to my knees to investigate. I flipped to double-check the title of the book. Sure enough, it was the one purchased from the bookshop. I paged through it. For a beginner's book, the spells seemed incredibly complicated. Some of them weren't even written in English.

"What are you doing down here?"

My head jerked up and I saw Ava standing at the base of the steps. Her pale face matched the fear in her voice.

"Looking for this." I held up the book. "I understand you used your mom's credit card to make a purchase at the local bookshop."

She hugged herself. "That's right. So what?"

I glanced back at the book. "This looks like you're trying to conjure a spell."

Ava forced a laugh. "A spell? Like magic? That's stupid. The book is a joke."

"Is the altar a joke too? How about the candle?"

Her expression crumpled. "You have no right to be down here. My mom should've told you no. It's my private space."

"Your mom is worried about you." I rose to my feet. "And rightfully so."

"I can't help it if bad things happen when I'm around. It's a coincidence."

I narrowed my eyes at her. "Do you know what bad things have happened here in Chipping Cheddar?"

She swallowed hard. "Something happened?"

I dropped the book and it landed on the altar with a loud thump. "Let's cut to the chase, Ava. You've been dabbling in things you don't understand and there've been consequences."

"What are you talking about?"

"Why did you target Chief Fox?" I demanded. "What happened? Did he catch you shoplifting or something?"

Ava's face grew beet red. "No, no. Something happened to the chief of police?"

"This is his pocket watch." I tapped the item on the altar.

She bowed her head. "Sometimes I take things without thinking."

"You're a kleptomaniac?"

Ava shrugged. "I guess."

"When did you take this from Chief Fox?" I asked.

"In the coffee shop," she said.

"You stole it out of his pocket?"

"No, he set it on the counter when he pulled money from his pocket. I took it when he was distracted. He didn't seem to notice that he'd done it."

"What were you trying to do with this book?"

Ava kneeled on the floor beside me. "Find my biological parents."

"Wouldn't the internet have been easier?"

Ava couldn't seem to meet my gaze. "I didn't want anyone to see my browser history. My parents monitor it to make sure I'm okay and not Googling how to dissolve boys' hair without leaving evidence." A small smile touched her lips.

"You used magic," I said.

"I didn't set out to make them bald," she said. "It was an accident. I only wanted to embarrass them so they'd leave me alone."

"When did you realize you could make things happen?"

"Probably when I was about six," Ava said. "At least that's when I realized that what I could do wasn't normal."

"Did you tell your parents?"

"Not exactly." Ava rubbed her hands anxiously on her thighs. "I started asking about my biological parents. I thought maybe that would help me understand myself better."

I shifted off my knees to sit on my bottom. "But your parents didn't like that, did they?"

She shook her head. "They freaked out. They said they didn't want me to track them down. That the adoption office sealed the records for a reason and I should be content with my life."

"So you kept quiet."

She fiddled with the pocket watch on the altar. "I felt like a bad seed from a rotten apple. I worried that if I told my parents about some of the strange things I could do, they'd want to give me up too."

I felt a pang of sympathy. It had to be difficult for her, trying to navigate a magical path all alone. She had no support. No knowledge.

"And you thought if you could locate your biological parents now, they might be able to answer questions about your abilities?"

She bit her lip and nodded. "There was no one else to ask without sounding crazy."

I squeezed her arm. "Ava, you're not crazy. You're a witch."

She tipped up her chin to look at me. "You believe in witches?"

"Kind of hard not to. My mother is one, so is my grandmother and her sister."

Fear and confusion marred Ava's smooth features. "Actual witches?"

"Yes. Listen, I'm going to tell you this because clearly you can keep a secret. Chipping Cheddar is full of supernaturals, but only humans with the Sight can detect us. To everyone else, we look like regular humans."

Her eyes widened. "All kinds of supernaturals? Not just witches?"

"Wizards, warlocks, vampires, werewolves, vengeance demons…"

Ava's mouth dropped open. "Demons?"

"There are different kinds of demons. Some are more primitive. Those you have to watch out for. That's my job. I work for an organization called the Federal Bureau of Magic."

"Are you a witch too?"

"No." I hesitated. As much as I hated acknowledging my true nature, I knew it was important to share it with Ava. "I'm something called a fury."

Ava stopped fiddling with the pocket watch. "I've read about those in mythology books. Aren't you supposed to have a hideous bird face?"

"Accounts vary." I leaned closer. "Do you see those weird-looking flames in my eyes?"

She peered into my eyes. "Wow. Those are cool."

"They're called the eternal flame. They're a sign of my immortality."

Ava choked on her response. "You're...immortal?"

"So is my stepmom, Sally. She's a vampire. She's perfectly harmless though. Organic blood smoothies made in a blender. That kind of thing."

Ava appeared to digest the information. "Why does this town have so many supernaturals?"

"There's an old portal here that doesn't function anymore," I said. "It's part of my job to check on it and make sure it doesn't open."

Ava hugged herself. "Where does the portal go?"

"Otherworld," I said. "The supernatural realm."

Ava laughed. "This is so crazy. I feel like someone is punking me. Where's the portal?"

"Do you know where the mound is?" I asked.

Ava nodded. "Some kids at school have mentioned it. Near the park, right?"

"That's the one." I paused. "There are other kids at school like you too. Meg's a werewolf. She takes after her mom."

Ava's face registered shock. "I sensed something about them, but I didn't know what it was. When I first met Meg at school, I felt connected to her, if that makes sense."

"It does. You aren't alone here, Ava, so I don't want you to feel that way. There are supernaturals here that can help you, even if they can't teach you magic."

Ava nodded. "Not alone. That would be a nice change."

"Now, I need to know which spell you did and what you used so I can help Chief Fox," I said.

Ava cringed. "What did I do to him?"

"You turned him into an actual fox," I said. "He's safe, but he needs to be restored to his human form."

"Is he...supernatural?"

"No, he's human, but he knows about us."

That fact seemed to relieve her. "He can have his pocket watch. I'm sorry I stole it."

My gaze flicked to the altar. "What else did you steal?" I picked up a locket on a fine chain and dangled it in the air.

"That belongs to a lady I met at the library. She was checking out a book and dropped her purse. Everything fell out, so I helped her pick it up."

"Except this." I popped open the locket and gasped when I saw the tiny pictures inside.

"What's wrong? Do you know her?"

Nausea threatened the contents of my stomach. "Oh, no. This is worse than I thought."

"I wasn't going to sell them," Ava said. "It's psychological. That's what one of my therapists told me. I don't handle stress well."

I stared at the picture. "This woman's name is Mrs. Langley and she's currently slithering around town as a venomous snake." I hesitated, not wanting to tell her the rest.

Ava covered her face with her hands. "I did that? Is she okay?"

"I honestly don't know." Now I really had to find that snake.

Ava blinked at me. "How do you know she's venomous?"

Great balls of fury. I couldn't lie to her, not now. "Because Mrs. Langley...the snake is responsible for the death of a woman."

Ava shrank back in horror. "No."

"I'm afraid so. A woman named Eloise Worthington. Her neighbor."

Ava began to cry. "I never meant to hurt anybody. It was an accident. I thought if I followed the spell in the book, I could find my parents and they'd explain why I'm so different."

"Show me the spell."

Ava turned the book toward her and flipped through the pages. "This one." She handed the book to me.

"It's in Latin," I said.

"I know. I used Google to translate it."

I squeezed my eyes closed. No wonder the spell went horribly wrong.

"I don't understand how I turned them into animals. I didn't even use their belongings as part of the spell," Ava said.

"Not intentionally," I said. "They were on the altar when you cast the spell. That's what happens when you're untrained." And using Google to translate. I thought about my own negative attitude toward FBM training and vowed to do better, or at least give Neville less attitude. It wasn't just bureaucratic nonsense. As a powerful fury, I was more dangerous than ten Avas combined. I owed it to everyone in town to have complete control over my abilities.

"What happens now?" Ava asked.

"Do you have a tote bag? I'm going to take this stuff to some witches I know and see if we can reverse the spell."

Ava jumped to her feet. "Do you need me?"

"I'm not sure yet. I'll let you know."

She went to a nearby closet and retrieved a burlap tote

bag. I shoved everything from the altar into the bag, including the book.

"Are they going to be okay?" she asked, her voice cracking.

I slung the bag over my shoulder. "I sure hope so." Because the alternative was too horrible to contemplate.

CHAPTER FIFTEEN

ON MY WAY to the LeRoux house, I stopped by the Havarti Rescue Center to borrow a cage.

"I'm not even going to ask what you need it for," Eileen said. She placed the cage on the counter and I was relieved to see it would be big enough for the snake.

"Thank you so much," I said. "I promise I'll bring it back in perfect condition."

"I know you will, Eden." Eileen slid the cage toward me. "I hear the chief isn't well. Do you know anything about that?"

"He should be better soon," I said. "He just needed bedrest."

"Don't we all?" Eileen said good-naturedly.

I carried the cage to the car and put it in the trunk before continuing to the LeRoux house. I'd already sent a text to let them know I'd made a breakthrough. Thankfully Corinne was able to leave her barista in charge of Magic Beans and meet us too.

Adele stood at the front door when I arrived. Her elegant fingers were slotted together as she watched me approach.

Despite her calm demeanor, I sensed the tension emanating from her body.

"Well?" she prompted.

I walked up the steps, carrying the tote bag. "Inside."

She turned and entered the house, closing the door behind me. Rosalie and Corinne sat at the round kitchen table wearing matching curious expressions.

"That's a big bag you've got there," Rosalie said. "I hope it's full of answers."

"You can say that." I produced the spell book and set it in the middle of the table. "It turns out that there's a new witch in town. Her name is Ava Milliken and she's in high school."

Adele blinked. "A new magical family moved to town? Didn't they register with the council?"

"No family. Only Ava is magical," I said. "Ava was adopted into a human family with no clue about the supernatural world. Her powers have been slowly growing over time and she's accidentally done this spell."

"How do you accidentally do a spell?" Rosalie asked.

"Oh, it's possible," Adele said. "I seem to recall you accidentally turning your fingers into sticks."

Rosalie bristled. "I was eight." She stretched out her hands to examine her fingers. "I was mortified. I had to wear long sleeves over my hands until I could figure out how to reverse the spell."

"Which you didn't," Adele gently reminded her. "I discovered the issue and did it for you. It was far too complicated for a girl your age."

"Ava was trying to find her biological parents, but she ended up turning Chief Fox and Mrs. Langley into animals." It seemed unnecessary to reveal the part about Ava's kleptomania. The girl had enough trouble on her plate right now and petty theft was the least of it.

"Wait," Corinne said. "Who's Mrs. Langley?"

I inhaled deeply. "The neighbor of Eloise Worthington."

"Eloise Worthington?" Rosalie repeated in a dismissive tone. "That woman's a complete nut job and, coming from me, that's saying something."

"Do I know her?" Corinne asked.

Rosalie snorted. "She's the one that protested in front of the Chinese restaurant wearing a hot dog costume because they gave her a crappy fortune in her cookie."

Corinne's face lit up. "Right. I've seen her around town. She cut me off at a light once. I only remember because she was wearing the hot dog suit at the time. It was so bizarre."

"The restaurant didn't want her out there protesting, so they offered her a month's supply of fortune cookies to make her go away." Rosalie hit the table with enthusiasm. "There was another time." She threw her head back and laughed. "Good Goddess, I'd almost forgotten. I watched her steal someone's parking spot that the other guy had been waiting for. Had his blinker on and everything. She drove right around him and took the spot. He laid on the horn and she just popped out of her car and gave him the finger before walking away. It was amazing."

Corinne clapped her hands. "She came into Magic Beans a few weeks ago. I had to ask her to leave."

Rosalie nudged her. "You told me about this. I didn't realize it had been Eloise."

"She bought a coffee and sat at a table, then proceeded to take off her shoes and clip her toenails."

"Was something wrong with her?" I asked.

"No, that's the best part." Rosalie smiled at her daughter. "Go on. You finish the story."

"When I asked her to leave, she said she was only doing it because she wanted the table by the window but it was already taken."

Rosalie laughed. "She sat as close to them as possible and

then tried to make sure the clipping came within range so that they'd get up and move and she could claim the table." Rosalie took a moment to enjoy the memory of the story. "I take it back. She's not a nut. She's my hero."

"Well, your hero is dead," I said. "The snake bit her."

Rosalie's smile faded. "That's unfortunate."

"Her cat is also missing," I said.

"Is there a chance that the snake…you know." Rosalie pretended to swallow something large.

"It's possible," I said, but I refused to give up hope. I was going to find Mischief and make sure she was brought somewhere safe. First I had to find the snake so that we could transform it back into Mrs. Langley.

"We're going to need Mrs. Langley and the chief before we can attempt to reverse the spell," Adele said.

"I know where the chief is," I said. "It's Mrs. Langley we have to find." I pulled Mrs. Langley's locket out of the tote bag. "I have something special of hers. I thought you could use it to locate her."

"Yes, we can certainly help with that, my dear," Adele said. She took the locket from my grasp.

"Is your family too busy?" Rosalie asked. Her sticky sweet voice didn't fool me. I recognized a witchy remark when I heard one.

"Rosalie, you know perfectly well that it's best not to involve them if it's not absolutely necessary." Adele looked down her straight nose at her daughter.

Rosalie gave me an appraising look. "What about you? You have powers."

I bit the inside of my cheek to keep me from saying what I really wanted to. "I prefer not to use my abilities unless I have to. There are consequences that I'd rather not face."

Rosalie clucked her tongue. "I'll never understand someone like you."

I folded my arms. "Someone like me?"

"Why don't we get started?" Corinne asked. I knew she was attempting to diffuse the situation, but I wasn't in the mood to tolerate Rosalie's attitude.

The middle LeRoux scowled at me. "You don't appreciate your gifts. You don't deserve to have them. Someone ought to do a spell and take them away. See how you like that."

"To be honest, Rosalie, I dream about a spell like that fairly often, but it would never work," I said. "The gods are pretty intent on their furies staying powerful. The more powers, the better, in fact. We're too rare to mess around with."

Rosalie got the message. She leaned against the back of her chair and regarded me coolly. "If you're so powerful, I guess we'll let you secure the snake."

"I'll help you," Corinne said. "We can't have a killer snake roaming around town."

"I doubt Mrs. Langley meant to kill Eloise," I said. We'd find out soon enough—hopefully.

Adele set a mortar and pestle on the altar and began to organize the necessary items. She lit a white candle and handed the locket to me. "Would you mind holding this over the flame, dear? Ready, witches."

As I held the locket, they joined hands and started to chant— "Winds of winter, hear our call. Sun of summer, hear our call. Bring us a vision to end it all."

An image materialized above the flame for all to see. "I see the snake," I said, my excitement rising. "She's near the ravine."

Adele blew out the candle. "Go now. Don't miss your chance."

Corinne twisted to look at me. "I'm happy to help unless you'd rather ask Neville."

"A witch is every bit as valuable as a wizard," I said. And Corinne was already with me.

Corinne beamed. "I'll bring a few items with me for spells, just in case."

"Bring the herbs for the trapping spell," Adele advised. "The snake can travel through places you can't. You need to be ready."

"Yes, Gran." Corinne gathered a few clusters of herbs from the organizer and tucked them into sachets.

"I'll drive," I said, as we left the house.

"Are you sure?" Corinne asked. "I think we've established who's the better driver."

"Except I would never let a hot dog cut me off." I smiled to let her know it was a joke.

"How's the chief?" Corinne asked, once we were settled in the car.

"As good as can be expected," I said. "At least he can talk now. It's reassuring."

"I have a feeling it's going to take him time to recover," Corinne said. "This whole thing must be a shock to his system."

I pulled out of the driveway. "I'm glad that he already learned about the supernatural world before this happened." I couldn't imagine the extent of the shock if he'd been wholly ignorant.

"I figured you came clean," she said. "I would've done the same."

"I appreciate that." It was nice to feel supported for a change.

"How did he react?" Corinne asked. "He must've been hard to convince. Someone with an analytical mind like his."

"I didn't want to tell him," I said. "He saw me dead and then he saw me alive." I shrugged. "There was nothing I could do."

"Did you have to report it to your superiors?" Corinne asked. "I imagine the FBM keeps track of civilians in law enforcement that know the truth."

I shifted uncomfortably. "I didn't file an official report." I did, however, tell someone in the FBM informally—Agent Quinn Redmond. I'd asked him how to handle the situation and he advised me to keep it under my hat so that the FBM didn't start throwing bureaucratic red tape around. As long as I trusted Chief Fox, there was no need to sound the alarm.

"You're protective of him." She nodded firmly. "Good. I thought you would be, but it's nice to know for sure."

When we reached the ravine, I pulled the car on the side of the road and parked with my emergency lights blinking. It was a thin stretch of road and it would be all too easy for another car to clip mine. I reached over and popped open the glove compartment to grab a flashlight in case I ventured into the woods. There were places where the trees were so close together that it seemed like the middle of the night.

"How do we convince a snake to come to us?" Corinne asked. She cupped her hands around her mouth. "Here, snakey snakey."

"I don't think so," I said. "Chief Fox said he can understand everything, so I think we should call her by name."

"I'm glad your family was able to get a speech spell to work," Corinne said.

"They use other methods," I replied, not mentioning the blood magic. "Ones I don't always approve of." Unfortunately, when I was desperate, I seemed to throw my integrity out the window. My mother liked to call me a hypocrite. I preferred not to think about that, although I secretly worried that she was right. If I was willing to resort to black magic when it suited me, how was I any better than they were?

I retrieved the cage from the trunk and carried it to the top of the ravine where I set it on the ground. I scrambled down the side of the ravine, shouting for Mrs. Langley as I went. Corinne ran to the opposite end of the ravine and copied me. A flash of movement caught my eye and I recognized the snakeskin pattern that I'd discovered in Eloise's yard.

"I see her!" Corinne's voice rang out.

"So do I." I motioned to the snake. "Mrs. Langley, if you'd please come to me, we can help you. I know you must be scared, but this is all a big mistake and we can turn you back into a human."

The snake stopped moving and I hoped that meant she was listening rather than preparing to strike.

"Mrs. Langley, this is Corinne LeRoux. I own Magic Beans. You're welcome to come in for a free drink whenever you like, if you'll just go to Eden. If you're not a coffee drinker, I have tea or hot cocoa with the small, pink marshmallows."

"You don't need to list the menu."

Corinne shrugged. "I don't want her to feel like I have nothing to offer her. Besides, it took me ages to track down the exact marshmallows I wanted. The whole town needs to know about them."

"I have a cage," I said loudly. "But I'm not going to keep you there. It's only to transport you safely to where we can turn you back."

"She works for the FBI," Corinne added. "She specializes in cases like yours."

Suddenly I remembered something that might help. I reached into my pocket and pulled out the locket. "I have something that belongs to you." I dangled the chain and the metal locket glinted in the light. "I bet you've been missing this. I saw the picture of your late husband in here. You must really miss him."

The snake inched toward me.

"That's right, Mrs. Langley," I said. "Come to me. I'm sure you miss your cozy bed too. I can help you get back there."

As the snake slithered along the side of the ravine, I heard the sound of crunching leaves to my left. I turned in the direction of the noise and saw the face of a Siamese cat.

"Mischief?" The cat meowed. "Mischief, why are you anywhere near this snake? It's too dangerous." Unless the cat had been trying to escape and the snake had been hunting her. The thought sickened me.

"What's going on?" Corinne called.

"Eloise's cat is here," I said.

"If we capture the snake, the cat will probably feel safe going back to her neighborhood," Corinne said. "You can always look for her there later and make sure she's okay."

She was right. As much as I wanted to help Mischief, right now the snake was the priority. I began to walk toward the cage. The door was already open and I was pleased when she slid inside without further prompting. Before she could change her mind, I shut the door and locked it. I had to imagine it was a relief to have someone recognize her and come to her aid.

"I can't see," Corinne yelled. "Do you have her?"

"Got her," I replied.

The witch hurried along the edge of the ravine, panting as she reached me. "Good work, Eden."

"Thanks for your help," I said.

"I meant it when I said we need to stick together. Our families may not want to work together, but that doesn't mean we can't." Corinne helped me lift the cage into the trunk and we returned to our seats in the car.

"To be fair, I don't want to work with my family either," I said. "The price is usually too high."

"I'm sorry. I wish it were easier." Corinne gazed out the

window. "Your life in San Francisco must've been so much calmer."

"I was working in the Organized Crime division of the FBI, so I wasn't exactly stress free." My shoulders relaxed slightly as I drove. "But you're right. It was calmer in its own way."

"It's family," Corinne said. "They have a way of magnifying each and every stress factor by a hundred."

"Look at Ava," I said. "Her adoptive family isn't even supernatural, but their relationship still pushed her to make rash choices that resulted in this mess."

"She's going to need a lot of guidance," Corinne said.

"Yeah. I was going to ask your family about acting as a surrogate coven for her. I certainly don't want to introduce her to my family."

"I think that's a brilliant idea," Corinne said. "Gran is an excellent teacher."

"And you'll be a good support system for her," I said. "She's been on her own and so confused. It must be awful for her."

Corinne cast a glance over her shoulder, toward the cage in the trunk. "Ava's not the only one. Someone's going to have to break the news to Mrs. Langley that she killed someone."

If her experience was anything like the chief's, then the chances were good that she already knew. My fingers gripped the wheel. Knowledge might be power, but it could also be a burden that some people weren't equipped to bear.

CHAPTER SIXTEEN

CORINNE and I carried the cage into the LeRoux house while Rosalie held open the door.

"That's one fugly reptile," Rosalie said.

"Careful," I warned. "She bites." I shifted the front of the cage so that it bumped against the witch and she jumped backward.

Corinne suppressed a laugh. "Did you make any progress on the reveal spell?" We set the cage on the floor and wandered over to the table where Adele had the contents of the tote bag spread across it.

"I'm afraid the spell can't be undone without Ava's involvement," Adele said. "She made it personal."

"What does that mean?" I asked. "Aren't all spells personal?"

"Gran means that Ava must've added a piece of herself," Corinne said. "Which means that Ava's the only one capable of undoing the spell."

"She was trying to find her biological parents, so that makes sense," I said.

Adele tapped the page in the spell book. "I can't believe

this child tried to translate a complicated spell like this with Google." She clucked her tongue. "We're fortunate that she didn't transform the whole town into animals."

"I'll drive over to her house now and get her," I said. "Should I meet you here?"

"The vortex," Adele said. "Our chances are better if we tap into the energy there."

"Got it." I left the house in a hurry and drove back to Burrata Street. Darkness had blanketed the town and my eyes took a moment to adjust to the change. Where had the time gone? It seemed like only half an hour ago that I was in the barn with Sawyer and Hugh.

I gave the front door of the Milliken house an impatient knock. Now that we were close to a solution, I couldn't stop thinking about Sawyer. The prospect of feeling his arms around me again was overwhelming.

"Agent Fury? That was fast." Relief flooded Rhonda's face.

"Fast?" I blinked in confusion.

"Well, I only reported Ava missing five minutes ago," Rhonda said.

My throat became dry. "She's missing?"

"Isn't that why you're here? I left a voicemail for the police. I thought maybe they transferred it to the FBI."

"When did you last see her?" I asked.

"Dinner. She was quiet. I could tell she was upset about something, but she wouldn't talk to me. I asked her about the drugs, of course." Emotions welled in her eyes. "She denied it. I wish she felt like she could trust us, you know. My husband is driving around looking for her, but his last text said he hadn't found her."

"I'll find her, Mrs. Milliken," I said. I had to—there were two innocent lives at risk.

"Thank you, Agent Fury. I appreciate your help. Ava's a good girl..."

I cut her off. "I know she is. And don't worry, after this, I'm going to get her the help she needs."

Rhonda sniffed. "It's inappropriate to hug a federal agent, isn't it?"

"I'm not much of a hugger anyway." An idea occurred to me. "Do you have an unwashed item of Ava's clothing that I could borrow?"

"Yes, of course. Whatever you need. I'll be right back."

I texted the witches to let them know I'd be delayed. I didn't have time for another locator spell. I was going to find Ava the old-fashioned way.

Rhonda reappeared with a white shirt bearing a cat face and the words 'Cat Person.' "Here you go."

"Does Ava have a cat?" I tucked the shirt under my arm.

"No, but she's asked for one many times. I'm not such a fan so I've put her off."

"You should get her a cat. Better yet, let her choose one." Maybe we could help find her familiar. "I'll be in touch."

The moment I returned to the car, my phone began to vibrate. "I'm in the middle of something important, Neville. What is it?"

"In that case, why am I not with you?" Neville asked.

"Ava's hiding and I need to find her so that we can reverse the spell."

"I can do a locator spell, my eternal ladyship."

I rolled my eyes at the moniker. "I know that, Neville, but I'm planning to use Princess Buttercup and track her the old-fashioned way. It'll be faster."

"I'm old-fashioned," Neville insisted. "I always offer to pay for the first date." He paused. "At least I would if I ever had one."

Now wasn't the time for lonely Neville to tug at my heartstrings. "We need to get on that, as soon as we're finished with Miss Escape to Witch Mountain."

"Yes, there's no need to worry about my well-being," Neville said. "You have much more pressing concerns."

"I'm worried about everyone's well-being here," I said. "It's sort of my job." I parked in front of the house and opened the car door. I wanted to whistle for Princess Buttercup and avoid stepping foot in the house, but I also needed the fox. Then I remembered the invisibility locket I'd stashed in the glove compartment. I'd been thinking I'd use it to sneak in and out of the chief's house for our romantic rendezvous, but this also qualified as a suitable occasion. I slipped the necklace over my head and opened the locket to trigger the charm.

Before I reached the porch, the hellhound came barreling out of the house, saliva flying in all directions. I opened the back door of the car and she climbed inside without hesitation.

"Stay here until I come back," I ordered.

I slipped into the house and snuck up to the attic to retrieve the fox. When I arrived, I saw Alice floating in front of the small television. She was watching an episode of *The Golden Girls* and laughing.

"Oh, Chief Fox. Isn't that Dorothy a hoot?" Alice said.

The fox couldn't hear her, of course. He only heard the television. At least it offered him some form of entertainment while he was trapped.

I closed the charm and came into view. The fox lifted his head, startled by my sudden appearance. "Eden?"

"Eden, why are you sneaking around?" Alice asked.

"Because I'm in a hurry," I said. I picked up the fox and huddled him against my chest. "I'm going to take you out of here now. Just stay quiet."

"Your boobs are really firm," he said, his tone muffled. "Are they supernatural?"

"This is not a good example of staying quiet." I crept

169

downstairs. "Anyway, my breasts have dense tissue. Nothing exciting."

"On the contrary," he said. "I'm finding them very exciting right now."

I pushed his nose out from between my boobs and hurried out of the house.

It wasn't easy to see in the rearview mirror with a hell-hound perched on the backseat, so I relied heavily on the side mirrors as I drove to the woods. I figured if I were Ava, that's where I'd go to hide. I parked on the side of the road and held Ava's shirt under the hellhound's nose.

"I need to find this girl, Buttercup," I said. "She's a young witch and doesn't know what she's doing, so no spewing acid at her."

The hellhound barked and nudged open the car door. I raced after her, not wanting her to get so far ahead that I lost sight of her. The scent of fresh pine and sea salt filled the air, triggering thoughts of the chief. Olfactory memory was fascinating to me. One sniff and I was back on the sofa in his living room, before his unfortunate transformation.

In the distance, an owl hooted and pulled me from my reverie. At least I hoped it was a real owl and not one of Ava's teachers. I drew a calming breath and shook my hands. *It's just a regular owl,* I reassured myself. In terms of personal items, the altar only had the chief's pocket watch and Mrs. Langley's locket.

It seemed that Princess Buttercup had sniffed every leaf and stick in the woods without success. The hellhound trotted back to me, her head hung in shame.

"No need to feel guilty." I kissed the top of her head. "You did a great job. The next time I need to track an escaped demon from Otherworld, you're on the team." I straightened as the realization hit me that there was another place Ava might go. A place she thought she belonged. "Come on, Buttercup. I think I know where to look."

Princess Buttercup galloped alongside me all the way back to the car. When I got there, I noticed a car with flashing red lights parked behind mine. A familiar figure peered through the windows.

I folded my arms. "Are you licking the glass?"

The deputy whipped around. "What? No." He grimaced. "Why would anyone lick the windows of your filthy car?"

"You tell me. You're the one with your face pressed against it."

Sean tried to maintain a professional demeanor. "Why are you parked illegally?"

My hands moved to rest on my hips. "It's the side of a deserted road Sean. Who cares?"

"I care," he said. "I'm in charge while the chief is sick and it's up to me to keep strict law and order in this town."

"Or what—it'll descend into chaos? Yes, my park job on the side of the empty road is destined to plummet us into a zombie apocalypse."

Sean glowered at me. "You're not above the law, Eden. I don't care how shiny that badge of yours is."

"I'm not trying to act above the law," I shot back. "I'm also not trying to act like a complete ass."

"I thought you were a kidnapper," Sean said. "I got a report about a missing girl."

"That's what I'm doing here," I said. "She isn't in these woods, but I think I figured out where she is. I'm headed there now."

He pulled out a pad and began to write me a ticket.

"Hey, what are you doing here? I just told you I'm searching for Ava too."

"I'm doing my job, Eden. It's nothing personal."

"You're ridiculous." I couldn't wait to get the chief back in working order.

Princess Buttercup growled at Sean for good measure and he took a step backward. "You should leash a dog that big," he said. "That's another ticket I can issue."

I patted the hellhound's head. "Great Danes are called gentle giants for a reason. She wouldn't hurt a fly...unless someone was getting on my bad side."

He placed the ticket on my windshield. "You can thank my generous nature that I'm only giving you this one."

I ripped the ticket from the windshield and opened the door for Princess Buttercup. The hellhound made a point of brushing her slobber on Sean's trousers as she passed him. I'd taught her well.

I slammed the door and sped off, deliberately spinning the wheels to spray dirt onto Sean's uniform. The immature part of me was pleased with the sendoff. I drove across town and parked across the street from Davenport Park. Princess Buttercup barked excitedly and wagged her tail when she spotted the park.

"I'm afraid we don't have time to play right now," I said. "Finding Ava is our priority." The hellhound trotted beside me as I made my way toward the hillside. "Stand guard and don't let anyone near here."

The hellhound barked once and I ducked inside the mound. Sure enough, Ava kneeled in front of the portal with her hands splayed on the wall. Her head turned at the sound of my entrance.

"What are you trying to do?" I demanded.

"Open a doorway," she said. "What does it look like?"

"Ava, you can't open a doorway to a dormant portal," I said. Certainly not with her level of power.

Ava turned back to the portal and closed her eyes,

appearing to concentrate. "You don't know. Maybe I can. Apparently I can do a lot of things I didn't realize."

I moved to stand beside her. "Why would you want to open the portal?"

"Maybe my parents are there. Maybe that's why they didn't keep me." Tears streamed down her cheeks. "They left me here because they wanted me to grow up in a safe place."

I placed a hand flat on her back. "If that's true, then why defy them? You have a good life here with your adoptive parents."

"I don't belong here," Ava said, her voice trembling. "I can't be trusted. Trouble finds me wherever we go."

"That's because you're a witch with human parents and no training," I said. "Under the circumstances, I think you've done remarkably well."

Ava wiped away the tears from her cheeks. "You do?"

"I can't imagine what it's been like for you, growing up with the knowledge that you can make things happen but not having anyone to ask for help or guidance." I crouched next to her. "You must feel very much alone." I fished a tissue from my purse and handed it to her.

She blew her nose. "I don't want to be a witch. I'd rather be human like my parents." She paused. "My adoptive parents."

"Ava, I realize how scary and confusing this must be for you…"

"I hurt those people," Ava said, and swallowed a cry. "I shouldn't have magic. I don't deserve it."

"Being a supernatural has nothing to do with whether you've earned it. It's the same as being born with brown hair or green eyes. It's just a part of who you are."

"I don't want it to be me," she said. "I don't want to be different."

"What you did to Chief Fox and Mrs. Langley was an

accident. You didn't know what you were doing. Do you think we all haven't experienced unintended consequences at one time or another? Human or not, we've all been there."

She sniffed. "You've…hurt people?"

I slid to my bottom and drew my knees to my chest. "I have. I almost killed my partner, Fergus."

"I thought it was Neville."

"Neville is my FBM assistant," I said. "Fergus was my mentor with the FBI. A human." I produced another tissue from my purse and gave it to her.

"I didn't realize you worked for the FBI."

"I don't anymore. They transferred me after the Fergus incident. I was too big of a risk."

Ava blew her nose again. "Why did you even want to work for the FBI when you have supernatural powers?"

I offered a rueful smile. "Because, like you, I decided I didn't want them."

"Why? If your family is supernatural too, why would you want to be normal?"

I didn't want to burden her with my own issues. "It's complicated."

Ava managed a smile. "Well, you still have a cool job. Federal Bureau of Magic sounds pretty awesome."

"It has its moments. You have to remember, though. The humans in town think I still work for the FBI. The cyber crime division."

"That's not as cool." She stuffed the tissues into her pocket. "Is there a way to get rid of my magic? Make me not a witch anymore?"

"I don't think you should make a decision like that in haste," I said.

"But it *is* possible?"

"One of my powers involves the ability to siphon magic from witches like you," I said. "If I can do that, I suspect there's a way to drain you of magic permanently."

Ava touched my arm. "How do we do it? Is it like an alien that sucks out my essence?"

I cringed. "No." I shook off her hand. "And I'm not siphoning anything from you right now. Not when you need to reverse the spell on Chief Fox and Mrs. Langley. You're the only one who can turn them back into people."

Ava's expression turned solemn. "I'm really the only one?"

"It's the way you performed the spell. It can't be broken by anyone else."

She appeared to digest this information. "That's pretty cool. I'm the only one in the whole world who can do this one thing."

"See? Being different can have an upside."

Ava stood and dusted off her knees. "Am I going to be in trouble for changing them?"

"No," I said, rising to a standing position. "I won't let anything happen to you. I promise."

"What about the chief?" she asked. "Are you sure he won't arrest me?"

"He won't," I said. "He'll leave you to me, I know he will."

"Because he's human and you're not?"

"Something like that." I didn't care to explain the complexities of our relationship to a teenager. Half the time, I couldn't explain them to myself.

Ava sucked in a deep breath. "What if I can't reverse the spell?"

I held out my hand. "I believe in you, Ava, and there will be witches there to help you. Experienced ones."

Ava placed her hand in mine and we left the portal together. Princess Buttercup waited for us outside and Ava started at the sight of her.

"What is she?"

175

"A hellhound," I said. "To everyone else, she looks like a Great Dane."

Ava extended a cautious hand. "Wow. A real hellhound. Can I pet her?"

"Yes, she's very friendly, unless you're Deputy Guthrie. She has standards."

Ava smiled as she stroked the hellhound's back. "She's beautiful." An idea seemed to occur to her. "If I gave up my magic, would I not be able to see her anymore?"

"I'm not sure," I said. "Maybe you'd still be a human with the Sight."

Ava nodded, mulling it over. "Do we need to break the spell at my house? Because my parents don't know anything and I don't think they could handle the truth."

"We're going to meet the LeRoux witches at the vortex."

"What's the vortex?" Ava asked.

"It's not far from here," I said. "It's a place where we can harness powerful magic. Since this is an important spell and you're young, we need the boost."

"Which way is it?"

"See if you can tell me," I said. "Close your eyes and reach for the magic."

Ava hesitated. "I don't know if I can."

"Yes, you can. The more you tap into your abilities, the less frightening they'll be to you." I felt like a hypocrite saying this, given that I avoided using my powers as much as possible.

Ava closed her eyes and pressed her lips together in concentration. "I feel a strong vibration."

"Coming from where?" I urged.

She turned in the direction of the vortex and pointed. "There."

"Well done. That's the right way."

Ava squealed. "Seriously? I got it right?"

"You sure did. There's a lot you can do, Ava, if you give yourself a chance."

She frowned. "If you're with the FBM, do you think you might be able to track down my biological parents?"

"I can't promise you anything, Ava, but I'll do my best."

Ava turned to face me, blinking away the teardrops that clung to her long lashes. "And what if you find them?"

I smiled at her. "I guess that next part is up to you."

CHAPTER SEVENTEEN

THE WIND HOWLED AS we climbed the hill to reach the vortex. The witches were there, along with the fox and the snake, which was still in her cage. They'd already drawn the magic circle.

"Welcome, Ava." Adele strode across the grass and clasped Ava's hands in hers. She kissed the teenager on each cheek. "My name is Adele LeRoux. This is my daughter, Rosalie, and my granddaughter, Corinne."

"I'm Ava Milliken." She gulped. "I'm a witch."

The LeRoux witches broke into laughter.

"Yes, I believe we've established that," Adele said, not unkindly.

"This is the vortex, huh?" Ava asked. "I feel a pull." She glanced at the ground. "It's coming from the ground."

"That's right," I said. "It's where ley lines converge."

Ava's eyes widened at the sight of the fox and the snake. She immediately hurried over to the fox and dropped to her knees. "I'm so sorry, sir. I didn't mean to do this to you."

The fox lowered his head. "I know, Ava. It's going to be okay."

Ava shrieked and fell backward.

"I probably should have mentioned that he can talk now," I said sheepishly.

Ava's gaze shifted to the snake coiled in the cage. "Both of them?"

"No, my family did a spell on the chief that gave him the power of speech," I said.

Ava turned to the snake. "I'm really sorry, Mrs. Langley. About everything. I never meant to hurt anyone."

"We should get moving," Rosalie said.

"Why? Is there a moon issue?" I asked, looking up at the sky.

"No, I'm supposed to meet a date for drinks," she said.

Corinne appeared slightly embarrassed by her mother's admission. I shot her a sympathetic look that said *been there, girl*.

"Ava, why don't you take your place in the circle and we'll guide you through the next steps," Adele said.

Ava hesitated before stepping into the circle. She approached the altar, seemingly entranced. "This one's nicer than mine."

"It should be," Rosalie said. "It was made by one of our ancestors back in New Orleans two hundred years ago."

I noticed two bowls of sand and a black taper candle, as well as the pocket watch and locket.

Ava placed her hands on the sides of the altar. "What do I do?"

"First you need to dig an outline of a man in one bowl of sand and an outline of a woman in the other," Adele said. "Then you light the candle and let the wax melt into the design of each bowl."

Ava glanced over her shoulder. "What about the animals?"

"They'll go in the circle with you," Corinne said.

The fox gingerly entered the circle and sat, while Corinne

pushed the cage across the chalk line.

"Once the outlines are filled with wax, I'll do a cooling spell so that the wax hardens into shapes," Adele said. "Then you can repeat after me."

Ava chewed her lip as she stared at the altar. "Okay, I'm ready."

The rest of us took a step backward so we were clear of the circle and let Ava begin the spell. Once the wax shapes had cooled, Ava scooped them out of the bowls and held one in each hand. A stark wind blew across the vortex, whipping my hair into my mouth. It tasted like coconut.

"Repeat after me," Adele said. She held her arms in a V-shape. "Winds of change, breathe new life into old shapes."

Ava held up the wax figures and chanted.

"I am grounded, centered, and ready to give back what was taken," Adele continued. "So let it be."

Ava repeated the chant. Light sparked from the wax figures and the animals began to twitch. They turned in a circle, so quickly that their forms became unidentifiable. By the time Ava lowered her arms, two people had joined her in the circle. Chief Fox was on his hands and knees, wearing the same clothes as when he'd transformed. Mrs. Langley's wrinkled face was pressed against the bars of the cage.

"Can someone help me, please?" the older woman asked.

Corinne rushed over to open the cage and helped Mrs. Langley escape her tiny prison. The older woman immediately vomited upon exiting the cage and narrowly missed Corinne's feet.

I ran to the circle, intending to embrace the chief. It was only when I crossed the white chalk line that I realized I had to be discreet. I shook his hand. "Good to have you back, Chief Fox."

He smirked. "Good to be back, Agent Fury."

Ava appeared on the verge of tears. "Are you both okay?"

Corinne checked the soles of her shoes to make sure she hadn't stepped in vomit. "I'm good."

"My back hurts," Mrs. Langley said. "And my joints are aching like crazy. I need my pills."

The chief stretched his arms over his head. "I'm much better now. Good job, Ava."

"How can you say that?" Ava asked. "I'm the reason you were stuck as a fox in the first place."

The chief moved to stand in front of her. "You didn't have to turn us back. You could've been so scared of getting in trouble that you refused to try, but you hung in there and made it happen. You should be proud of yourself."

Ava's lips parted. She seemed uncertain how to respond.

"Does everyone know I turned into a snake?" Mrs. Langley asked. "My children must be worried sick."

"They don't know, Mrs. Langley," I said.

"I suppose it would be too much for them to take in," the older woman said. "To be perfectly frank, I'll probably collapse later from a stroke. I've been trying to stay calm this whole time, but it hasn't been easy. I won't even watch television programs with supernatural influences. I didn't even like Caspar and he was meant to be a friendly ghost."

"You've done very well, Mrs. Langley," Adele said. "And we promise you won't have a stroke later. There are precautions we intend to take." She gave me a pointed look and I understood.

"I don't think my neighbor will agree that I've done very well," Mrs. Langley said with an abrupt laugh. "Eloise tried to hit me with a baseball bat." The older woman touched her lips. "I think I might've bit her."

Ava stifled a cry and the chief and I exchanged uneasy looks. Someone had to tell her the truth. I stepped forward, but the chief cut me off.

"Mrs. Langley, I'm afraid you did bite your neighbor," he

said.

The older woman laughed. "She deserved it. She's been a thorn in the side of our neighborhood since the day she moved in, but everyone's too afraid to say anything to her. At least she won't know it was me. I don't need her dancing on my front lawn in her hot dog suit."

I shifted my weight from foot to foot, waiting for the chief to drop the bombshell.

"Mrs. Langley," he said, "Eloise won't be dancing in her hot dog suit anymore."

"That's a relief. Did someone finally take the horrible thing away from her?"

"Not exactly."

"Eloise is dead," Rosalie blurted. It seemed that her date was more pressing than the need to be tactful. "You killed her."

Mrs. Langley' seemed to take a moment to process the news. Her shaking hand covered her mouth. "I killed her?"

"You were a poisonous snake," Rosalie said.

"Venomous," I corrected her.

"I remember that we got in a fight," Mrs. Langley said. "She tried to hit me with a baseball bat and I only wanted her to help me."

"In fairness, Mrs. Langley, she didn't know it was you," I said gently. "She thought she was being attacked by a snake." Because she was.

The older woman touched her teeth. "I didn't realize I was venomous. I was only trying to protect myself. It was all so confusing. Like a distorted nightmare."

I gave her arm a reassuring squeeze. "It must've been awful for you. I'm so sorry."

Her hazel eyes met mine. "What does this mean? Am I under arrest?" She glanced at the chief. "Will I spend the rest of my life in prison? Granted, it won't be long given my current state, but still. I would've liked to spend more time with my grandchildren."

"I don't think this falls under my jurisdiction," the chief said. He cut a glance at me. "What do you say, Agent Fury?"

"What happened to Eloise Worthington stays right here on this hill," I said. "I won't be filing a report with my agency."

"She was killed by a snake in a freak accident," Adele said. "That's the official story."

"I have something that belongs to you," Ava said. She brought the locket to Mrs. Langley and hooked it around her neck.

The older woman gasped. "I thought I'd lost it. My husband gave it to me for our anniversary before he died. It's very precious to me."

Ava handed the chief his pocket watch.

"Thank you," he said. "This means a lot to me."

Ava glanced between them. "I swear I'll never steal anything ever again. No more kleptomania for me."

"You probably won't," Corinne said. "If the stress and anxiety of hiding your true nature triggered your kleptomania, maybe it'll be reduced now that you've accepted your magic. It was probably the fact that you were fighting it that created emotional development issues."

Rosalie's brow creased. "You sound way too smart. No wonder you're having trouble attracting men."

Corinne and I groaned in unison.

I looked at Ava. "What do you think? *Have* you embraced your true nature?"

Ava's eyes sparkled. She seemed energized by the reversal spell. "I think I have." Her gaze shifted to Adele. "Will you help me so that I don't screw up again?"

Adele reached out and clasped the girl's hand. "It would be our pleasure, dear."

I faced the chief. "Will you call Sean and let him know that you're better and you found the missing girl?" I asked. "I've had enough interaction with him this week to last the rest of the year."

The chief chuckled. "No problem." He motioned to Ava. "We should get you home before your parents lose their minds." He looked at me. "We'll catch up later."

"I can drive you," Corinne offered. "Your car's still at your house."

"Mrs. Langley, Agent Fury will drive you home," Adele said.

The older woman didn't seem bothered. "Which way is your car, dear?"

"Down the hill near Davenport Park. Can you walk that far?" I asked.

Mrs. Langley nodded. "It will feel good to walk on two legs."

I took her by the arm and guided her through the darkness. Princess Buttercup waited patiently by the car.

"Oh, I love Great Danes," the older woman said.

I opened the door and let the hellhound jump into the back. Mrs. Langley sat in the passenger seat, humming softly. I got behind the wheel and sent a quick text before joining the road.

When I pulled into Mrs. Langley's driveway, Sally waited in front of the house. I parked and told Princess Buttercup to stay put.

"Oh, the air's turned chilly all of a sudden," Mrs. Langley said, as she opened her door. "Oh, hello. I didn't see you there."

"Mrs. Langley, I'd like you to meet my stepmom, Sally."

Mrs. Langley nodded. "A pleasure, Sally. Do you know I was a snake?"

The vampire looked directly into the older woman's eyes.

"You will not remember anything that happened to you from the moment you became a snake. You will not remember that you had anything to do with the death of Eloise. You will not remember that supernaturals exist."

Mrs. Langley nodded absently. "I will not remember."

Sally smiled, showing her fangs. "Good luck to you."

Mrs. Langley seemed to come to her senses. She looked around her yard. "Hello, who are you? Why am I outside at night?"

"I was lost and asked you for directions," I said. "You were kind enough to help me."

"Oh, good." Mrs. Langley smiled. "I like to be helpful." She walked to the front door and let herself inside.

Sally and I stood beside my car. "Thanks," I said. "Sorry about the short notice."

"It's no problem. How's the chief?"

"Pretty good, all things considered." I opened the door and slid into the seat.

"Do you need me to erase his memory too?" she asked.

"That won't be necessary," I said. "The council has agreed to let him in on our secret."

Sally fixed me with an anxious look. "I like him, Eden. I really do, but have you forgotten that you're immortal? That you're dangerous?"

I tightened my grip on the wheel. "I'm not dangerous to him."

"Maybe not deliberately, but you're dangerous all the same."

"He's the chief of police," I said. "His job has its own dangers."

The vampire leaned against the car in frustration. "Eden, darling, I will never try to tell you how to live your life."

"No, that's my father's job."

She bit back a smile. "Indeed."

185

"I don't want to think about my immortality on the best of days, so I certainly don't want to ponder it in connection with the chief."

"Does anyone else know about you two?" Sally asked.

There was no point in denying it. I could tell that she knew. "No family," I said. "And I'd like to keep it that way. You want to talk about dangerous, that's where the real problem is."

"I don't disagree with you there." Sally stared into the darkness. "I love you, Eden. I don't want to see you hurt."

"Sawyer won't hurt me."

"Not with his actions, no," Sally said. "But his human nature is enough to cause you irreparable harm. He'll only be young and handsome for so long and then what?"

I laughed. "You think I'll ditch him at the first sign of grey hair?"

"No, of course not," she said. "I only mean that there will come a point when it's clear that one of you is aging and the other isn't."

"So I'll be the Paul Rudd in our relationship," I said.

"I don't know who that is," Sally said.

"You should. He's awesome." I heaved a sigh. "Listen, Sawyer knows all about me and he accepts it. I can't ask for more than that. The rest we'll need to navigate as it comes. We only recently started dating. It might not last a year, let alone a lifetime. Look at my parents. They thought they'd be together for their lifetimes and the marriage didn't even last a human lifetime."

"Beatrice's loss was my gain," Sally said.

"They're better off apart," I said. "I agree with that."

Sally looked at me. "Do you really think it's that fragile that you won't last a year?"

"No," I admitted. Anyone who could digest the amount of crazy information I'd thrown at him and still want to get involved with me was unlikely to break up with me because I chewed with my mouth open or some other random habit. Not that I chewed with my mouth open. That was gross.

"Just protect yourself," Sally said. "That's all I ask."

"I've been protecting myself my whole life," I said. "It hasn't really worked out for me. I think taking a chance with Sawyer is a step in the right direction."

Sally reached into the car and patted my shoulder. "I want to see you happy and so does your father. You deserve it."

"Then you'll promise not to tell him about this," I said.

She hesitated. "You know I don't like keeping secrets from your father. Secrets aren't healthy for a relationship."

"Maybe not, but it's the only way my relationship is going to survive. You know my family. They get wind of this and you'll be erasing the chief's memory next and shipping him back to Iowa."

"Is that where he's from? I thought it was Idaho."

"That's potatoes. He's corn."

"Right." Sally's eyes glimmered in the moonlight. "I'll keep your secret for now, Eden, but eventually you'll have to come clean."

I knew she was right. I just wasn't ready to face it yet. "I promise."

I put the car in reverse and backed out of the driveway quickly so she couldn't see that my fingers were crossed. The relationship was too new to put it under my family's magical microscope. They'd hex both of us before I could utter the word 'boyfriend.' I drove home, thinking about Ava. It was both encouraging and strange to see how she'd embraced her supernatural side. I was older and more experienced, yet I still struggled to come to terms with my identity on a daily basis. At some point, I needed to accept it. Maybe, like Ava, if I stopped fighting it, my life would improve.

There was only one way to find out.

CHAPTER EIGHTEEN

ON SATURDAY MORNING, I stood in front of the barn with John Maclaren, carpenter of dreams. The doors were closed and the handles tied together with a wide red ribbon.

"I thought we'd do this with a flourish," John said. "Do you want to call your family so they can witness this miraculous event?"

I raised my eyebrows. "Are you serious?"

"Yeah, good point. I don't need your mother making suggestive comments about wrapping me with ribbon so she can untie me."

I smirked. "You know her so well."

John gestured to the doors. "Should I have brought a pair of giant scissors?"

"Nope. I can handle it." I tugged one end of the ribbon and the knot relaxed.

"Welcome to your new home, Eden."

I crossed the threshold and a wave of excitement threatened to overwhelm me. My new home. No more mattress in the attic. No more lack of privacy...Well, sort of.

"John, it's amazing. Thank you so much." My gaze traveled around the barn, noting the many details I'd been unable to see throughout the renovation. There'd been too many tarps, drop cloths, beams, and tools everywhere, so this was the first time I was seeing the barn in its unblemished state. Wide-planked flooring. Exposed beams. Soaring ceilings. He'd even installed a stone fireplace that looked like it belonged in a Swiss chalet.

"You've outdone yourself," I said. "I had no idea this was such a diamond in the rough."

"Don't stand here gawking in the great room," John said. "Come and see the kitchen."

"That's what we're calling this space?" I asked.

"You can't call something this stunning the living room," John said. "It deserves better."

He wasn't wrong. I followed him to the back of the barn where I admired the custom wood cabinetry and soapstone countertops. Light, bright, and airy, just the way I envisioned it. I gasped at the sink.

"What's wrong?" he asked.

"Nothing. I just realized that I've reached the age where I'm excited about an extra wide sink."

He chuckled. "You're still a little young for that, but it's a testament to your excellent taste."

"Aunt Thora is going to want to move in with me so she can commandeer my kitchen." I wasn't worthy of these appliances. I was going to have to take lessons from Rafael and earn my place here.

"Plenty of room if you want that," John said. "You've got the master bedroom plus two more."

I was so giddy, I felt like I could float upstairs.

"Hello? Anybody home?" The sound of the chief's voice lifted my spirits even higher.

John and I returned to the great room to greet him.

"This place is something else," the chief said, scrutinizing the height of the ceiling.

"It's been the best project I've had in a long time," John said. "I appreciate the opportunity."

"Let's go upstairs," I said. "I'd like to see my bedroom."

"I was going to suggest that," the chief said with a wicked grin.

I flashed him a menacing look as we climbed the open staircase to the next floor where the gallery landing overlooked the great room.

"I can see Olivia and Ryan getting into trouble up here," I said. I pictured them throwing their toys over the railing to the room below. Teddy bear overboard!

"You wouldn't have had anything like this in San Francisco, would you?" the chief asked.

"Ha! Definitely not." I stopped short when we reached the master bedroom. The room was magnificent with more exposed beams and plenty of natural sunlight through the large windows. "This place was worth the wait." For the first time in a long time, I felt fortunate, even though I fully recognized I'd made a deal with the devil in order to live here. My parents each paid half of the renovation costs and I'd be paying rent, as well as living a stone's throw away from them because the barn sat directly on the border between their two properties. Hopefully my new home wouldn't come at too high a cost.

"Do you have any furniture?" the chief asked.

"That's next on the list," I said. "And I know a good place to start."

"I'm glad you're happy with everything," John said. "You deserve it, Eden."

"I'm going to miss seeing you around all the time," I said. It felt like the end of an era.

"I still live in Chipping Cheddar," John said. "You're welcome to come by whenever you feel like it."

The chief cleared his throat. "Well, I think she'll be pretty busy furnishing this place and keeping up with her job. Lots of cyber crime happening out there. Online fraud is a constant battle."

I bit the inside of my cheek to keep from laughing. Chief Fox's mild display of jealous was more adorable than I would've expected.

John shook my hand and then shook the chief's. "I've got an appointment, but give me a call if you have questions about anything."

"Thank you so much. I know living here will be amazing." I hoped.

I listened as John made his way across the landing and back down the steps. Once I heard the click of the double doors, I squealed with delight.

"This place is mine," I sang, and performed a fairly uncoordinated happy dance to accompany my words.

Chief Fox laughed. "Someone's in a good mood."

"Can you blame me? You're back to normal. I can move out of the attic and not worry about passing my mother in the hallway in the middle of the night in her lingerie. Everything's coming up Eden."

He slid his arms around my waist. "You also helped a teen witch. You saved Mrs. Langley. You've had a busy week, Agent Fury."

"I'm glad Ava is going to work with the LeRoux witches," I said. "She needs to learn how to practice magic responsibly."

"Wouldn't it be better to ask your family?" the chief asked. "They seem more powerful than the LeRoux family from what I could see."

"They are, but I try to keep them out of supernatural

affairs," I said. "They don't always make smart choices." That was putting it mildly.

"They can't be all bad," he replied. "You turned out okay."

Despite them, not because of them. I needed to change the subject before I said too much. "What about Eloise's cat, Mischief?" I asked. "Any luck finding her?"

He shook his head. "Sean canvassed the neighborhood, but she hasn't turned up."

Although I was disappointed, at least I'd seen her alive. She'd come back to the neighborhood eventually. "That reminds me. Sean gave me a ticket when I was searching for Ava."

His mouth twitched. "Yeah, I saw that. Don't worry about paying it."

"I can't ignore a ticket. It'll go on my record."

"Not if the ticket never made it into the system, which it didn't." The chief kissed the tip of my nose. "I'm not letting him punish you for doing your job."

"I don't want special favors," I said. "That's how we get into trouble." I placed my hands on his cheeks and enjoyed the rough texture of his stubble against my skin. He clearly hadn't shaved since turning back into a human.

He curled his fingers around mine. "What's wrong? A second ago, you were living your best life."

"Trust me, I am." I sighed. "It's just that when you were a fox, there was this moment where I thought maybe you were a secret shifter and I realized how much easier our lives would be if you were."

"Because we wouldn't need to sneak around?"

"Basically."

He released my hands. "Do the FBI regulations not apply if the chief of police is a supernatural? Somehow I doubt that." He peered at me. "Are you sure you're not disappointed that I'm a boring human after all?"

"There's nothing about you that's disappointing or boring, Sawyer, except maybe the fact that you sound vaguely Canadian sometimes. I just wish it could be easier."

"Some things are worth the trouble though, right?" he asked. I detected a slightly hopeful tone and hated that he felt the need to question it.

"One hundred percent," I said. I edged into his arms and rested my cheek against his chest. "I wouldn't change a thing about you."

"Ditto. Wings and flaming eyeballs and all. Say, there's something I've been meaning to ask you," he said. "When I first turned into a fox, you said 'they won't get away with his.'" He inclined his head. "Who'd you mean by 'they?'"

I cleared my throat, struggling for a good answer. "My family likes to get into mischief and sometimes they cross the line." Cheese and crackers, that had to be the lamest lie I'd ever told.

"Why would they target me?" he asked.

"I thought maybe they found out about us and wanted to teach me a lesson."

He pulled back slightly. "By turning the chief of police into a forest animal? That's not what I would call mischief."

"Well, they weren't the responsible party, so it's all good," I said, wishing this conversation would end. I didn't want my family to know more about the chief and I didn't want the chief to know more about my family. Sally's words came flooding back to me—*secrets aren't healthy for a relationship*. Maybe not, but sometimes they were necessary. Ignorance was safest when it came to the dark side of my family.

The chief studied me. "Do I need to be concerned about your family—as the chief of police, I mean?"

"No," I said quickly. "They mostly inflict harm on each other." Or me, depending on their moods. "They don't like other people enough to get involved with them."

"Sounds like some people I know back in Iowa."

"I doubt that very much."

He kissed me firmly on the lips. "And while we're on the subject, I don't think you bring trouble because of your true nature, but I definitely think trying to hide it makes things worse."

I peered at him. "What are you talking about?"

"Back when I was a fox in your attic…" He stopped and chuckled. "Never thought that was a sentence I'd utter. Anyway, when I was a fox, you said that you bring trouble wherever you go because of your true nature. It isn't being a fury that's problematic. It's the fact that you resist who you are. It was true for Ava and it's true for you."

"It's sort of necessary given that I live in the human world," I said. "Can you imagine how people would react if they knew the truth?"

He squeezed my waist. "Like me? With patience and understanding?"

"They wouldn't and you know it. They'd be scared to death. They'd want to burn me at the stake. That's what we do to things we don't understand. We attack. It's human nature."

"I think you underestimate us," he said.

"Trust me, Sawyer. You're the exception and not the rule."

"Then maybe think about it differently than you have been. Don't worry so much about other people and whether or not they'd accept you. Focus on accepting yourself first and the rest will follow."

"I'm a work in progress, Sawyer."

"Aren't we all?" He took my hand. "Let's go downstairs. I'd like to see the kitchen where you'll be cooking my gourmet meals."

"What?" I asked with such force that he burst into laughter.

He pointed at me. "You should see the look on your face. Priceless."

I cupped his rugged jaw in my hand and squeezed. "Rule number one of having a supernatural girlfriend. Don't aggravate her for your own amusement."

"Or what? You'll shoot those flames from your eyeballs and extinguish me?" He threaded his hands through my hair. "What's rule number two?"

I tipped back my head to see him better. "Kiss her often. Because she deserves to be kissed by someone who knows how."

A slow smile spread across his face. "I think I can manage that."

Interested to know where Mischief the cat ended up? Check out Divine Place, my supernatural cozy mystery series. Book 1 is called *Murder and Mahjong* and you can order it here.

For more Federal Bureau of Magic, keep an eye out for the next book—Every Picture Tells A Fury.

ALSO BY ANNABEL CHASE

Thank you for reading *Hell Hath No Fury*, the 7th book in the Federal Bureau of Magic series. Sign up for my newsletter and receive a FREE Starry Hollow Witches short story— http://eepurl. com/ctYNzf. You can also like me on Facebook so you can find out about the next book before it's even available.

Other books by Annabel Chase include:

Starry Hollow Witches

Magic & Murder, Book 1

Magic & Mystery, Book 2

Magic & Mischief, Book 3

Magic & Mayhem, Book 4

Magic & Mercy, Book 5

Magic & Madness, Book 6

Magic & Malice, Book 7

Magic & Mythos, Book 8

Spellbound Paranormal Cozy Mysteries

Curse the Day, Book 1

Doom and Broom, Book 2

Spell's Bells, Book 3

Lucky Charm, Book 4

Better Than Hex, Book 5

Cast Away, Book 6

A Touch of Magic, Book 7

A Drop in the Potion, Book 8

Hemlocked and Loaded, Book 9

All Spell Breaks Loose, Book 10

Spellbound Ever After

Crazy For Brew, Book 1

Lost That Coven Feeling, Book 2

Wands Upon A Time, Book 3

Charmed Offensive, Book 4

Urban Fantasy

A Magic Bullet

Burned

Death Match

Demon Hunt

Soulfire

Spellslingers Academy of Magic

Outcast, Warden of the West, Book 1

Outclassed, Warden of the West, Book 2

Outlast, Warden of the West, Book 3

Printed by Amazon Italia Logistica S.r.l.
Torrazza Piemonte (TO), Italy

13646893R00116